TROUBLE at the
TANGERINE

Also by Gillian McDunn

TROUBLE at the
TANGERINE

Gillian McDunn

BLOOMSBURY
CHILDREN'S BOOKS
NEW YORK   LONDON   OXFORD   NEW DELHI   SYDNEY

BLOOMSBURY CHILDREN'S BOOKS
Bloomsbury Publishing Inc., part of Bloomsbury Publishing Plc
1385 Broadway, New York, NY 10018

BLOOMSBURY, BLOOMSBURY CHILDREN'S BOOKS, and the Diana logo
are trademarks of Bloomsbury Publishing Plc

First published in the United States of America in April 2024
by Bloomsbury Children's Books

Bloomsbury books may be purchased for business or promotional use.
For information on bulk purchases please contact Macmillan Corporate and
Premium Sales Department at specialmarkets@macmillan.com

Library of Congress Cataloging-in-Publication Data
Names: McDunn, Gillian, author.
Title: Trouble at the Tangerine / by Gillian McDunn.
Description: New York : Bloomsbury Children's Books, 2024. | Audience: Ages
8–11. | Audience: Grades 4–6. | Summary: Eleven-year-old Simon is ready
to make the Tangerine Pines his forever home, but when a robbery occurs
in the apartment building, he and his new friend set out to solve the
case and keep his family from moving again.
Identifiers: LCCN 2023028224 (print) | LCCN 2023028225 (ebook) |
ISBN 9781547611003 (hardcover) | ISBN 9781547611010 (e-book)
Subjects: CYAC: Moving, Household—Fiction. | Apartment houses—Fiction. |
Stealing—Fiction. | Mystery and detective stories. | LCGFT: Detective
and mystery fiction. | Novels.
Classification: LCC PZ7.1.M43453 Tr 2024 (print) | LCC PZ7.1.M43453 (e-book) |
DDC [Fic]—dc23
LC record available at https://lccn.loc.gov/2023028224
LC ebook record available at https://lccn.loc.gov/2023028225

Book design by Jeanette Levy
Typeset by Westchester Publishing Services
Printed and bound in the U.S.A.
2 4 6 8 10 9 7 5 3 1

To find out more about our authors and books visit
www.bloomsbury.com and sign up for our newsletters.

For Gauri

Very few of us are what we seem.
—Agatha Christie

TROUBLE at the
TANGERINE

another version of home

Simon Hyde's parents were the kind of people who felt most at home when they were *not* at home.

"Why settle for ordinary? The Hydes are searching for *extraordinary*," Dad was fond of saying. "To find that, you can't stay in one place."

Simon had placed lobster traps in the Atlantic and roped cattle on ranches and squeezed into the lofts of tiny homes. He'd snowshoed through the Rockies, zip-lined through treetops, foraged for mushrooms, and dived off cliffs.

But there was one thing that Simon had not experienced. He had never had a real home. A forever home. The kind of place where he knew all his neighbors. A place where he had lots and lots of friends.

For the past eleven years, the family had moved from one part of the country to the next, each time traveling in their ancient vehicle, Vincent Van Go—Vincent for short. If someone charted their routes crisscrossing the map, it would look like a connect-the-dots page gone absolutely berserk.

Their adventures were documented on his parents' social media account, The Hydes Go Seek. It had started back when Simon was a baby, just as a way for friends and family to keep up with their activities. But their following had exploded over the years. Now, just over a million strangers had a bird's-eye view into the life of Simon and his parents each week.

They went to amazing places. But no matter how perfect the scenery—no matter how *extraordinary* the adventure—it was only a matter of time before his parents became restless.

"Wouldn't you like to live on a houseboat, Simon?"

"Did you know it's possible to see the northern lights from certain parts of Idaho?"

"If we lived in a cabin, you could take a snowmobile to school."

"I've always wanted to live somewhere with blueberry bushes in the backyard."

Together, they'd lived in twenty-six different places— twenty-seven if you counted Tuscaloosa, which Simon did not. He barely remembered it. They'd stayed only three weeks before moving to Kalamazoo. They'd only lived *there* for only eight months before moving to Pensacola. And so on and so on.

So far, each version of home had ended the same way. After a time, they'd say goodbye to classmates and neighbors. Then they'd pack up Vincent and drive to the next version of home. Each move meant another school. Another set of friends. Another chance to be the new kid.

It was summer, and the Hydes were moving again. But this time was going to be different. This time, Simon was going to find his forever home. Even if his parents didn't know it yet.

CHAPTER 2

the plan

Simon liked to have a plan.

Plans do not have to be complicated. In fact, some of the best plans are simple. Such was the case for Simon's plan for moving to a new place—his two-part, top-secret system he called Code Name Chameleon.

Code Name Chameleon, Part One: Blend in.

In nature, camouflage is key. Things that stand out tend to get noticed. Things that get noticed tend to get eaten.

The rules were the same for new kids. Simon did not want to be noticed. He *definitely* did not want to be eaten. So the first step was to make sure he did not stand out in any way.

In Abbottsville, blending in meant playing soccer and wearing tall, solid-color socks.

In Chase Park, it meant marching band and specially tied shoelaces.

In Brookton, it meant skateboards and striped shirts.

In Owens Grove, it meant chess championships and blue hair.

In Cape Piddo, it meant surfing and friendship bracelets.

The proof of his success was clear. Simon was never the person with the most friends, but he had also never been eaten.

Code Name Chameleon, Part Two: Don't be weird.

Deep down, Simon was a kid who loved rocks and gems. A kid who would spend entire days reading adventure and fantasy books. The one who hated heights. The one whose stomach tied up in triple knots every time he moved.

Were these things all that unusual? Maybe not. But it was safer to keep those parts of him squashed down until he got to know a new place. The squashing stage was supposed to be temporary—eventually, he'd have friends who saw him for exactly who he was.

At least, that's how the plan was *supposed* to work. The problem was that as soon as Simon's new-kid status started to fade, it seemed like his parents were already planning their next move. They called themselves "digital nomads"— between the money that their social media presence made and their regular jobs, which were computer-based, they could work from absolutely anywhere.

Even as they'd planned for the move to Rigsby, Dad had eyed Simon's things.

"Remember, we have to travel light."

Simon knew the requirements by heart: he could only take what could fit in Vincent. Two medium boxes. One backpack. But there was one additional thing that was absolutely nonnegotiable: his rock collection.

He turned sideways to hide the size of the box. "I already packed my bag and boxes."

Dad raised an eyebrow. "What's that you're holding?"

Simon clutched his collection protectively. "It's just one small piece of every place we've ever lived."

Dad looked skeptical. "Some people would say that carrying rocks from place to place is the exact opposite of traveling light."

Simon narrowed his eyes. "*Some* people would say that my collection would be smaller if we moved less often."

At this, Dad had rumpled his hair and grinned before walking away. He thought Simon was joking. But Dad didn't know about Simon's super-top-secret plan. The one he called **Operation Rigsby**. This was the plan his parents knew nothing about. It had three simple steps, and Simon had already completed the first two.

Step One: Find the perfect town. Simon had investigated and researched. He read so many top-ten lists that he began to see them in his dreams. He did Google Street View until his eyes felt like sandpaper. Until he found the perfect place. A city that was not too big and not too small. A city that was just right, with a bustling downtown and plenty of bike paths and public transportation to make Dad happy. For Mom, he wanted museums, farmers markets, and proximity to the beach and mountains for their day-trip adventures.

Step Two: Move there. He'd printed out multiple top-ten lists about the city's restaurants and bookstores and parks and coffee shops. He sent his parents links to video tours and pertinent posts. Before he knew it, his parents were starting to talk about how fun it would be to move to Rigsby.

Step Three: Stay there forever. This was the most important part—and also the most complicated. He'd have to keep an eye out for any signs of restlessness. He'd have to make sure his parents truly loved every part of their new city.

Because Simon wasn't looking for another version of home. This time, he was looking for the real thing.

CHAPTER 3

a forever kind of feeling

"You have arrived," the voice on Mom's phone chirped as Vincent groaned to a stop in the apartment building's loading zone.

Mom patted her pants pocket. "I've got the keys right here. Why don't I go ahead and unlock the apartment? Maybe I'll grab a few pictures for The Hydes Go Seek on the way in."

Simon brightened. "I'll start unloading."

Mom and Dad exchanged glances.

"What?" Simon asked. "I can handle a cross-country move with one hand tied behind my back."

Dad scratched his head. "You have to admit it's a little more challenging with a busted fibula."

Simon frowned, staring at his bright green fiberglass

cast, which was hoisted across Vincent's backseat. A broken leg—his souvenir from the last town they lived in, when he'd decided to ignore his fear of heights and try to climb a tree. Everything had been fine until he looked down and his brain had become a spinning pinwheel of dizziness. After that: a quick fall, followed by a loud *crunch.* Then: a summer spent in a cast.

Dad caught his eye. "You can sit in the back and hand me what I need. That would be really helpful."

Simon reached for his crutches, smiling to himself. He clambered out of the van, swiveling his head to take in their new street—the steady streams of cars and bikes commuting to work, a city bus roaring past, the scent of fresh bread from the corner bakery curling around him. Rigsby felt *alive.* Simon had a good feeling about this place. A forever kind of feeling.

As he circled to the back of the van, Mom was snapping photos for The Hydes Go Seek. Then she hurried up the steps. She placed a brick to prop the front door and disappeared inside the building, which was just as it had looked online—five stories tall and made of yellow brick, with arched windows and a deep orange roof. To the left of the door was a sign that read TANGERINE PINES.

Dad followed Simon's gaze, squinting at the building. "What's that supposed to mean?"

Simon tore his eyes away from the bustle of the city. "Hmm?"

Dad pointed at a sign. "Tangerine Pines—an odd name, don't you think? One, there are no tangerines. Two, there are no pines. Three, there are no *tangerine pines*, whatever those are."

Heat crept up the back of Simon's neck. He wanted Dad to like this place—to really like it. Making fun of the building name was a bad way to start out.

He cleared his throat. "It's just a name. It doesn't have to be anything deep."

Dad scratched his head. "We've stayed in places with corny names before. It's usually not a good sign. Remember the Rose Petal Apartments?"

Pictures didn't always tell the whole story. Sometimes listing photos were accurate, and sometimes they stretched the truth a little. When they'd picked up the keys for the Rose Petal, the Hydes discovered crumbling pink stairs, a swimming pool overflowing with slippery green algae, and, to top it all off, a rowdy family of skunks that had taken up residence in the primary bedroom. In that case, the truth had been stretched a *lot*.

"Come on," Simon said. "Those little skunk babies were cute."

Dad grimaced and continued to rummage through the van.

"Rigsby is going to be perfect," Simon said. "I just know it."

He continued to look around. Even though he didn't want Dad to criticize their new home, he actually *did* think names should have significance. It was reassuring to rely on logic and order and answers. Everything meant something. It was just a matter of knowing the right place to look.

To the left was a much larger building, which towered over the Tangerine Pines. Made of modern metal and cool glass, a sign with sleek lettering read THE LOFTS ON HIGH STREET. That was a clear, straightforward name.

Then he turned his head to the right. This building was slightly smaller than the Tangerine Pines but more impressive, with white brick, lush green topiaries, and gleaming red doors. Its corners were sharp, its paint was crisp, and the uniformed man out front had exceptional posture.

He tilted his head in its direction. "There's no sign on that one."

Dad hefted two boxes in his arms and made for the stairs. "That's not an apartment building—it's a house."

Simon let out a low whistle. "A house? More like a *mansion*. They have their own doorman!"

Dad was already halfway up the steps. "I think the Tangerine was originally a single residence but was converted into apartments at some point. That doesn't explain the goofy name, though."

Dad continued up the steps. When he reached the front doors, he wedged his foot in the gap and swung it open to create enough space for him to step through.

Simon leaned against the van, studying his surroundings. Even though he'd been anticipating their move to Rigsby for months, it felt completely different to be there in person. The traffic was steady—cars, trucks, and buses. A delivery bike gracefully swerved around the van. Even on the sidewalks, people seemed to move with purpose. Dogs on leashes stayed with their owners and didn't stop to sniff. Babies in their strollers had determined expressions as they crammed cereal puffs into their tiny mouths. The trees in front of the building were dotted with pink flowers, like they had been decorated specially for their arrival.

Even above the noise of the street, Simon heard her before he saw her.

"Incoming!" A two-wheeled scooter careened down the sidewalk. On top of it was a tall girl with medium-brown skin and dark hair with a streak of turquoise—no. Seafoam green. A green bird perched on her shoulder.

The bird squawked. "Incoming! *Incoming!* Who's a pretty baby? Who's a pretty boy?"

They whooshed past. Then the girl cut the scooter wheels left to dodge a pedestrian and then at the corner turned right, vanishing from view.

Simon looked around. In some places, a girl and a bird riding a scooter would be noteworthy. But here, no one seemed to blink an eye. He smiled to himself. This was going to work out just fine for the Hyde family. A warmth spread through him. His plan had come together perfectly.

If only the boxes could float up the stairs and unpack themselves. He ached to be settled as soon as possible. Balancing on one leg, he swung the backpack onto his shoulders; then he hobbled toward the stairs, taking them one at a time. Simon couldn't wait until he got his cast off. He would never take walking up a flight of stairs for granted again.

He was halfway up the stairs when he heard a voice.

"And just *what* do you think you're doing? Are you trying to get the whole building robbed?"

CHAPTER 4

an unpleasant welcome

Simon was so startled, he almost toppled down the stairs.

In the doorway of the apartment building stood an older white man with a gray handlebar mustache. He wore a paint-splotched coverall with stitching above the left chest pocket that read OSCAR. The added height from the steps combined with the scowl on his face made him seem like he was a giant.

Simon gulped. "I don't want anyone to get robbed!"

Oscar glowered. "We never prop doors. An open door invites trouble. You're not trying to let in some of your hooligan friends, are you?"

Simon's mouth dropped open. They'd only just moved there—he didn't even *have* any friends. And if he did, they wouldn't be *hooligans*.

"I'm really sorry," Simon said. "I didn't know."

The man squinted. "You're moving into 3B? Last name Hyde?"

Simon pointed at Vincent. "My parents are unloading boxes while I watch our van."

At this, Oscar came to the top of the stoop. He wore a pair of thick-soled shoes that squeaked with every step. "I'm the super." He pulled a rag from his pocket and wiped his hands.

Simon leaned on his crutches and took a deep breath. It was too early to be off on the wrong foot with someone in Rigsby—especially someone in charge of his new building. He put on his friendliest smile. "I'm Simon."

Oscar made a vaguely disapproving clicking sound with his tongue. "You're in the city now, kid. You can't invite crime in the front door like that."

Out of the corner of his eye, Simon realized that the girl with the scooter was riding past again. She still had the bird on her shoulder. This time, she slowed as she passed, like she was trying to overhear the conversation.

Simon flushed. "I was watching the whole time. No one went in or out."

Oscar snorted. "What would you do about it anyway— a pip-squeak like you."

"I'm eleven and a half," Simon said sharply.

"Like I said, a pip-squeak," Oscar replied. "With a broken leg, no less. A kid can't keep a whole building safe. This is the city! There's crime everywhere out there." He peered suspiciously up and down the street.

Simon followed his glance. It seemed like a normal-enough street. He shrugged. "I'll be more careful."

Oscar squinted. "One more thing—your family has been receiving mail at this address for weeks, even though your lease didn't start until today. That's considered bad form, just so you know."

Simon looked at Oscar sideways. This didn't sound right at all. Simon loved plans and systems, and the Hydes' relocations were always done fastidiously and exactly. When they were between addresses, everything was forwarded to his parents' assistant, who scanned any important documents. Mom and Dad wouldn't want papers piling up before they arrived.

Simon was tempted to tell Oscar how wrong he was, but he swallowed his arguments and instead put on his extra-polite smile. "Sorry about that. I'll definitely pick it up just as soon as we move in."

Oscar waved his hands impatiently. "See that you do."

The apartment building door swung open, and Dad stood there for a moment, glancing between Simon's face and Oscar's. He took two steps toward them.

"Thomas Hyde," he introduced himself, reaching out for a handshake.

Oscar hesitated, then slowly offered his hand in return. The walkie-talkie on his hip squawked, but he ignored it.

Dad nodded. "Is there a problem?"

"Everything's fine," Simon said quickly. "There's a rule against propping the door open, but it's fixed now."

Oscar made a noise that sounded like *harrumph*. He turned to leave, shoes squeaking with every step. The double doors closed solidly behind him. Simon breathed a sigh of relief.

Dad looked at him. "Not the friendliest guy, huh?"

Simon shook his head. "He was acting so mad over nothing." He was about to explain about the mail, but then Dad started speaking again.

"Oh well," he said. "If this move doesn't work out, we have a backup plan."

Simon's frowned. "We do?"

Dad's eyes twinkled. "Before we decided on Rigsby, I thought we should take a yearlong road trip. Just think of it—we could explore for a while, then get in Vincent and drive somewhere new. We'd never spend more than a day or two in the same place."

Simon suddenly felt dizzy. He lowered himself to the porch steps, trying to keep his expression neutral.

"What about work?" he asked.

Dad shrugged. "We could work evenings. Or I could work when Mom is driving and vice versa."

"And school?" Simon's voice felt scratchy.

"We could always homeschool. It didn't work out that well before, but we could try it again."

No. No, no, no. Absolutely not. Homeschooling was really great for some families, but their one experiment, when Simon was in fourth grade, could be termed Code Name Disaster. Didn't Dad remember the fractions frustrations? Didn't Mom remember the drama of diagramming sentences? That's not even counting the forgotten moldy cheese science experiment that had fallen under a seat in the van and made Vincent stink for weeks. The memory made Simon's stomach clench.

"But we just got here. We haven't even unpacked!"

Dad reached over and mussed Simon's hair. "It's just an idea—but I think it would be really fun. New people, new places . . . what's not to love?"

Whistling, Dad took the steps two at a time and retrieved another set of boxes from Vincent.

Simon swallowed hard. One thing at a time. First the van would be unloaded; then they'd all go upstairs together and unpack. For dinner, they'd order takeout and then play a silly game like charades. This was a move-in-day tradition, and as far as Simon was concerned, it was one of the best parts about arriving in a new place.

He tried to smile as Dad walked past him, heading back into the building. Oscar's "welcome" had felt like a rough start. Simon would have to work extra hard to convince Dad about Rigsby being a good place. He closed his eyes and took a deep breath.

Then he felt something push against his leg.

Something warm. Something wet?

He opened his eyes. A pair of brown eyes looked back. A medium-size shaggy dog was sitting at his feet, panting. She licked his ankle and beamed at him.

"Help! *Help!* Somebody grab Bianca!"

CHAPTER 5

a pleasant welcome

Even from half a block away, the woman's voice carried over the street noise.

"*Bianca!* Grab her, please!"

Simon reached for the dog's collar, but she didn't have one. If Bianca made a break for it, there would be very little he could do—with his broken leg, there was no way to chase after her. But she seemed content to sit next to him as long as he scratched behind her ears.

When the woman arrived at the steps, her cheeks were flushed, and she was a bit out of breath. She pushed her red curls off her face and smiled at Simon. She was definitely a grown-up, but not a super old one. Simon figured she was in her late twenties or thirties—around the age of his favorite babysitter from six moves ago.

She tucked a long strand of hair behind her ear. "Oh, thank you! I'm so glad you stopped her. We were out for a little walk, and then she slipped off her lead."

He ducked his head. "It's no big deal."

The woman's eyebrows drew together. "It *is* a big deal. She might have kept on running if it hadn't been for you. I've only had her for a week—she doesn't know the building yet."

She continued talking as she reattached a sparkly pink collar. "I help take care of stray dogs with a rescue organization—that means lots of animal friends in and out. The collar was too loose because I forgot to adjust it from the dog I had last time."

"So she won't stay with you, then?" Even though Simon had just met her, he was already disappointed to know she was a temporary resident at the Tangerine Pines.

"Only until she has her puppies," the woman said.

Now that she mentioned it, Simon noticed that the dog's belly was bulging. She rested her head on his knee.

The woman smiled. "Bianca seems to be a big fan of yours. Usually she gets nervous around new people."

Bianca looked up at him with soft brown eyes. Simon rubbed the scruff around her ears. "She seems friendly."

The woman nodded. "I think she's been extra cautious

because her maternal instincts have already kicked in. It will be nice for her to have her puppies in a home and not a shelter, but she's struggling to adjust to busy city life."

Bianca looked back and forth between them, shaggy tail wagging as if she knew she was being discussed. Even though her coat looked wiry, it was actually very soft. Simon gently patted her back.

"She's a nice dog," said Simon.

"I agree." She fastened the collar around Bianca's neck. "I've grown attached to her in a short time. I even renamed her—the rescue had called her Petunia. But everyone in my family has names that relate to a color, and I thought she should have one, too."

Simon looked at her blankly.

"Bianca means 'white' in Italian," she clarified. "And my hair is red, so—Ginger." She struck a little pose, kicking her leg out to the side. Simon had to laugh.

As she moved, the sun reflected on her necklace, which was made of red and white gemstones. In the light, it didn't just sparkle—it seemed to glow.

Simon's eyes widened. "Whoa—what kind of necklace is that?"

Ginger's eyes darted back and forth. She touched the necklace once, then again before answering.

"They're rubies and diamonds," she said finally. "It's

very old, and it even has its own name . . . it's called the Magnificent. I inherited it from my great-aunt when she died."

"I love rocks—I collect them," Simon blurted. "It looks like something out of the minerals and gems exhibit at the Smithsonian."

At this, Ginger smiled, patting the necklace again. "Some people think a thing like this should be locked up in a safe, but I think it's better to enjoy wearing it. At least, that's what my great-aunt would say."

"I'm Simon." He nodded in the direction of Vincent over in the loading zone. "We're just moving into 3B."

She clapped her hands excitedly. "So you'll be living at the Tangerine? You must come visit Bianca again. She needs to socialize."

At her words, the building doors swung open, and Simon's parents joined them on the steps.

Bianca stiffened and started to bark.

"See?" Ginger said to Simon. "I told you she isn't sure about new people."

"It's okay, Bianca—that's my mom and dad." Simon spoke in a low voice. The dog quieted at his words, almost like she understood him.

Ginger's eyes widened. "Remarkable!"

Dad grinned at Bianca. "Who do we have here?"

The adults introduced themselves, and Ginger explained how Simon had helped with the runaway dog.

"He acted very quickly," she said. "And with a broken leg! That's one nice and responsible kid you have there."

Mom grinned at Simon. "Agreed."

Ginger smiled, adjusting one of her bobby pins. She seemed to be the exact opposite of Oscar. It was good to know that there would be at least one friendly face in the apartment building.

"He's a natural with dogs," Ginger added. "I know the rescue organization will be seeking forever homes for Bianca and her puppies. If your family is interested, I could connect you."

Simon's heart lifted. His parents had always said no when he asked for a pet, but maybe they would feel sorry for Bianca and her puppies.

"Can we? *Please?*" he asked.

Dad shook his head. "The way we move around so much wouldn't be fair to a pet."

"We don't *have* to keep moving around," Simon said.

There was an awkward pause while the adults exchanged looks.

Mom patted his shoulder. "I'm sure Simon would love to spend some time with Bianca if she'll be around for a while." She looked carefully at Ginger. "Your necklace is gorgeous, by the way."

Ginger hesitated before answering. "Thank you—I was just talking to Simon about how it used to belong to my great-aunt. The family story goes that she was briefly engaged to a prince. They never got married, but she kept the jewels anyway. She was a bit of a collector—and more than a little eccentric."

Simon found that interesting. Ginger seemed a little quirky, too, now that he thought of it.

"It almost seems like it could be a piece in a museum," Mom said.

Simon grinned. "That's what I said!"

Ginger cleared her throat. "I should probably let you finish moving in. If you need anything, I'm in 2B, which is exactly one floor below you."

"Is it okay if I come visit Bianca?" Simon asked.

Ginger smiled. "You're welcome anytime. There are quite a few people on vacation right now, so it's quieter than usual. Hopefully you'll find some kids to make friends with soon enough."

"Thank you," Dad said.

"I'll drop by later with a welcome basket," Ginger said. "I always like to share a few local items with newcomers."

Bianca barked again, and Simon turned his head to

see what was bothering her. It was the girl with the scooter.

"I like your cast," she said without stopping. "That color is spectacular."

"Oh my goodness," squawked the bird. "Oh my goodness!"

They continued down the street before Simon could respond.

"Better get you inside," Ginger murmured to Bianca. "Good meeting all of you."

A woman with a runaway dog and a scooter-riding girl and parrot. It seemed like life would be interesting at the Tangerine. Simon couldn't wait to find out.

a new home

Simon had seen all kinds of apartment buildings, and the lobby was always a hint as to what the rest of the building would be like.

Some were grand, with enormous crystal chandeliers and marble floors that echoed when someone walked across them. Some were shabby, with worn carpet, dim lights, and peeling paint. But the Tangerine Pines lobby was neither grand nor shabby. It was . . . *unusual*.

He closed his eyes and breathed in deep. The lobby smelled of books, cinnamon, and vanilla—exactly like someone was baking a pie inside of a library. He opened his eyes again. Facing the front doors was a portrait of an old woman. She sat in a chair with a very straight back and held a gray cat on her lap. Her eyes were brown and seemed to smile, even though her expression was stern.

Before Simon could ask who she was, Mom was pointing at a room off the main lobby.

"They call this the conservatory," she said. "Isn't it wonderful?"

The room had wide windows, bookshelves, and leafy green potted plants. It felt cozy but bright, like the perfect place to spend an afternoon.

Mom ran her hand along a wall panel with an elaborate design. "Look at this gorgeous fretwork."

Simon frowned. "What's that?"

"It's the name for this type of carving," Mom answered. "See how the wood is cut in these elaborate patterns? The gaps are backed in mesh. It probably took a ton of time."

Simon nodded, continuing to look around the room. In one corner was a fireplace covered in penny tiles that had been glazed in a variety of jewel-colored tones. There was one plum-colored velvet sofa and four squashy armchairs. Most of the shelves were stacked with books, but one held an assortment of puzzles and jigsaw games.

Dad caught his eye. "It's one of the common areas that all the residents can use. There's also a courtyard in the back with a garden. We can't go see it yet because Oscar is painting back there, and the doors are taped off.

Maybe we can check it out after dinner or sometime tomorrow."

As they walked to the elevators, his parents filled him in on some other facts about the building. There was no doorman—which was possibly why Oscar had been so upset. Everyone entering had to use a key or be buzzed in. Even though Simon would be using the elevator until his cast was off, there was also a set of stairs—plus fire escapes on the outside of the building, which Dad said were only for emergencies.

"There are four floors of apartments—sixteen in all," Mom said. "The laundry and mailboxes are in the basement—we'll show you that later."

Oscar had been so intense about 3B's piled-up mail. Simon made a mental note to look for it when he visited the mail room, if it existed at all—he had his doubts.

Inside the elevator, Dad pressed "3." The family was quiet. As excited as Simon was, there was always an amount of nervousness associated with seeing a new home for the first time. But before long, the elevator chimed, and they exited onto the third floor.

He took a moment to get his bearings. From the elevator, they turned right and then right again. Dad pushed open the door, and they went inside.

"What do you think?" Mom asked.

Simon made a disappointed face. "I was hoping there'd be some baby skunks."

Mom laughed and squeezed his arm. Dad snorted.

Simon maneuvered around a pile of boxes to check out the entire space. The Hydes usually tried to rent apartments that were at least partially furnished. Sometimes the furniture they inherited was crummy and worn out. But this time, it looked comfortable and tidy. The kitchen was old, with a vintage yellow stove. But it had a decent amount of space and an efficient layout, which Simon knew was important to Dad.

Simon tilted his head toward the kitchen. "It's going to be a lot easier cooking here than with Vincent and the camping stove."

Dad drummed his fingers against one of the speckled counters. "I'd much rather make our meals under wide-open skies. But this will do."

"Do you want to pick your room?" Mom asked, changing the subject. "One has office furniture and the other has a bed, but we can easily swap them."

Simon weighed both options carefully before deciding. The first room—set up with a computer desk and a small filing cabinet—was larger and had a whole wall of storage cubbies. But when Simon pulled open the curtains, he saw that the windows faced the building next door, which seemed boring.

The second room was smaller and L-shaped, with a roof that slanted on one side. Its closet was tiny, but Simon didn't mind. There was a bookshelf, a solid-looking bed, and even a dresser. He had recently gained a new appreciation for dressers. It wasn't easy to use a closet when balancing on one leg.

But the best part of the room was all the windows: one that led to a rickety-looking fire escape, one that was small and square, and a bay window with a seat that fit right inside and a view of the courtyard below. He circled the room so he could examine it closely—the bottom dresser drawer with a chipped knob, the light switch with a small moon sticker, the floorboard by the closet that made a distinctive *krr-squeak* when it was stepped on. He loved every bit of it.

Simon grinned at his parents. "This one."

Mom smiled back. "That's what I guessed."

Dad stood in the doorway, stretching his arms and yawning. "I'm exhausted all of a sudden. I think I'll order our dinner."

He disappeared into the living room. Simon couldn't shake the feeling that Dad wasn't happy about their move to Rigsby.

"Is there something wrong with Dad?" Simon asked.

Mom sighed. "Nothing major. I think he's still day-dreaming about the big road trip he hoped to do this year."

Simon swallowed. "But we just *got* here. We haven't even unpacked! Why do we always have to be thinking about the next place?"

She shrugged. "Sometimes picking one path makes you think about all the wonderful things you'd get to do if you took the *other* path. This is just his way of settling in. He'll be okay."

Simon nodded. He wanted to believe her. She stepped into the living room and returned with a stack of boxes. "Do you want help with your boxes?"

He shook his head. "I can handle it."

Mom smiled. "Even with putting away your clothes?"

Simon pointed at the dresser. "I'll put everything there—no hangers."

"Oh!" Mom said, eyes widening. "I just thought of something."

She pushed a wheeled desk chair into Simon's room. "This might help with getting around if you want a break from the crutches."

Simon sat in the chair and spun in a circle. "Thanks, Mom." She smiled and left the room.

He pushed from one corner of the room to the other, each time grabbing an armful of books before scooting back to the shelves. He emptied the first box after several trips, then started moving stacks of clothes to the bureau.

He bumped his leg on the side of the bookshelf a couple of times as he launched himself around, but at least he didn't have to worry so much about keeping his balance.

Simon slipped his phone from the pocket of his athletic shorts, which were stretchy enough to fit over the cast. He pulled up The Hydes Go Seek. One by one, he swiped through the images.

Swipe. Mom, Dad, and Simon perched at the edge of a vast canyon. It was pristine and untouched—by all appearances, it seemed that Simon and his parents were the only humans for miles. Of course, the camera angle avoided the snaking line of cars waiting to enter the park, the hikers jostling elbow to elbow, and the fact that heights made Simon feel like losing his lunch.

Swipe. A swirly pink-and-purple sunset melted over a crystal lake. The caption didn't mention the clouds of biting flies that had attacked every inch of their exposed skin, which oozed and crusted for days afterward.

Swipe. Simon chomped a famous roadside diner's triple-decker cheeseburger, dripping with special sauce. Not shown (or, thankfully, *smelled*): his forty-five-minute trip to the bathroom that had taken place shortly after he finished the last mouthful.

Simon sighed, returning the phone to his pocket. Sometimes the gulf between perfection and reality loomed especially large. To anyone looking at the pictures, their life was perfect and full of adventure. But all Simon wanted was a chance to settle down.

He wheeled the chair over to his bookshelf and opened the box that contained his rock collection. He spread them out on top of the bookshelf and looked at each one.

Usually, holding the rocks made him feel calm—like each one was an anchor to a place they'd lived, a version of Simon that had existed. He had turquoise from New Mexico and a garnet from New York. He had jade from Wyoming and rose quartz from South Dakota. He had several Petoskey stones from Michigan, which was really fossilized coral. He loved their textures, colors, and shapes. Whenever he felt alone, he could touch them and remember who he was.

But that day, Simon felt restless. He pushed himself to the bay window and studied the courtyard. Oscar was painting the steps to the building. He looked much less intimidating from a distance. The rest of the courtyard contained a few trees, scattered garden furniture, a storage shed, and a stone fountain. Maybe the whole building hung out there for barbecues and events. Simon liked that—it felt friendlier than when they lived in the suburbs and everyone had their own fenced yards.

Simon turned back to his room. Unpacking had gone

quickly—maybe more quickly than it should have for a normal eleven-year-old. Dad liked to brag about how they could pack up all their things within an hour. But Simon wondered what it would be like to have more stuff. He'd known families who kept every piece of art, every assembled LEGO set, every board game they'd ever played. In their previous town, Simon had visited a neighbor kid who showed him the desk he kept in his room. The boy had carved his initials onto the desk next to another set of initials—the one his dad had carved when *he* was a boy.

Simon's brain froze when he saw those initials together. It felt like the same feeling Simon would get when he was working on a computer and the system paused while the wheel spun, like it was trying to get a little more energy to do what was asked of it. Simon's brain simply could not compute the idea of a single item—a *large* single item—staying in his family for that long.

He definitely could not imagine what it would be like to live in one place. What would it be like to go to the same school for longer than a year? What would it be like to stick around long enough that he would see *other* new kids come in?

Simon loved his parents, who always said that their little family of three was all they needed. For his whole life, they'd been adrift like a clump of dandelion seeds. But Simon wanted it to take more than a gentle breeze to move them along.

It was like every time they reached a new place, there was a countdown clock clicking away until it was time to move again.

It was almost like he could hear that clock. *Tick. Tick. Tick.*

Simon shook his head, as if to clear it. The sound came again, more insistently this time. So it wasn't his imagination.

But was it a *tick-tick-tick* or a *click-click-click*? Or a *tap-tap-tap*?

The sound was coming from the fire escape.

the visitor

Simon pulled back the curtains from the rear window.

He had not known what to expect from the ticking, clicking, tapping sound. But he had *definitely* not anticipated a person outside his window.

The girl he'd seen earlier had her hand outstretched, about to tap again—but when she saw Simon, she stopped and waved.

Her wide smile showed a dimple in each of her round cheeks. In her hair, she wore a star-shaped hair clip.

"*Mnn mmoo mmmen mmis?*" she asked, her voice muffled through the glass.

Simon unfastened the latch. As soon as he cracked it open, she began to speak.

"Are those rocks?"

She was looking over his shoulder at his collection. Simon's stomach dropped. The rules of Code Name Chameleon clearly stated that his love of rocks was *not* the first thing a kid should learn about him. Sometimes people thought rock collecting was babyish or awkward.

But it was not like he could lie about the pile of rocks that she was peering at.

"Um," Simon said. "Yes?"

The girl tilted her head thoughtfully. "Rocks are interesting. I like interesting things."

Simon didn't have time to think through all the Code Name Chameleon rules, so he just shrugged. "Me too."

She nodded crisply, as if that matter was settled. "I probably should introduce myself. Greetings and salutations. I'm Amaya and I'm eleven."

"I'm Simon. I'm eleven, too."

Amaya clapped her hands as if she'd just won a lifetime supply of candy. "I thought we would be around the same age. Where did you live before here?"

He paused. Sometimes it almost felt easier to list the places he *hadn't* lived than the ones he had. "We move around a lot."

Amaya nodded sympathetically. "That must make it hard to make friends."

Simon frowned. She was right—it *was* hard to make

friends. But he'd barely met her. He didn't want her to feel sorry for him. Code Name Chameleon Step One was about blending in—not about looking desperate.

"It's okay," he said. "I always make lots and lots of friends. They had a big going-away party for me before I left."

He swallowed hard. This was stretching the truth. His school had an end-of-year event for all the fifth graders, not specifically for him. He decided to change the subject. "How exactly did you get up here?"

Amaya shrugged elaborately, pointing. "I used the ladder—super easy."

Simon looked upward, counting at least thirty-nine steps before a wave of vertigo made him shudder. Heights and Simon didn't get along—that was putting it mildly. Looking at the view from a window was one thing, but the fire escape seemed rickety. Its floor was a metal grate, which meant that if Simon stood there, he could peek through the holes and see about fifty feet of air beneath him. No thank you.

Amaya scooted to the side to make room. "There's plenty of space if you want to come out here, too."

Simon pointed to his leg. "The last time I tried being up high somewhere, I got this souvenir."

He replayed the scene in his head. At his old school,

it seemed like everyone climbed the big silver maple on the last day of classes. All he wanted was to be just like everyone else—so he'd held his breath and climbed. Everything was fine until he looked down.

Simon didn't remember falling. But he remembered the sickening crunch as he smacked the ground.

He remembered *plenty* of what happened next: the ambulance ride to the emergency room with his worried parents, the X-ray tech's sharp intake of breath when seeing "the exceptionally unlucky break," and the solemn tone of the doctor when she said, "Six weeks in the cast *minimum*—maybe more."

Amaya looked sympathetic. "At least you were able to get a really good color. I like that green."

Simon paused. "Do you want to come in?" He wasn't sure what the right manners were for someone who suddenly appeared outside another person's window.

Amaya shook her head. She separated out the seafoam-green streak of her hair and began to braid it. "I'm good—I love the fire escape, and it's so nice out tonight. But thank you for the invitation. I'll come in next time," she added.

Simon's eyebrows rose. "Next time?"

She looked at him as if he had grown two heads. "*Of course* next time. We're going to be friends: we have to be.

There aren't many people our age around, you know. The big glass building mostly has people who haven't had kids yet. The Tangerine Pines has mostly younger kids. The only person our age is Calvin Morris, who is my literal archenemy." She made a disgusted face.

"What about that big, fancy house next door?" Simon still felt curious about the house—mansion—with its doorman and sharp edges.

Amaya twisted the earring in her left ear. "They keep to themselves pretty much."

There was an awkward pause. As the silence grew, Simon ran his mind backward, searching for what he had done wrong. Blend in—check, at least he thought so. Don't be weird—well, maybe it was weird to care too much about the neighbors immediately after moving in.

Simon leaned against the windowsill, trying to look casual. "So . . . where's your bird?"

He grimaced. That question had sounded better in his head. But Amaya didn't seem to care.

"Ezekiel? He belongs to Professor Quintana, who's one of my clients."

Simon's eyebrows popped up. "Clients?"

Amaya rummaged in a messenger bag with a big glittery star on the outer flap and unpacked the following items:

- A ring with at least a dozen keys and one pink-haired plastic troll
- A tiny replica of a lifeboat
- A container of bubbles
- A paperback thesaurus
- A notebook and pencil
- A phone
- A walrus that seemed to be made of squeezy stress-ball-type material

She frowned faintly. "I know they're here somewhere. Oh!" She held up a small red box. "Can I interest you in a shriveled grape?"

Simon blinked. "A shriveled *what?*"

"Some people call them raisins, but that's marketing. I prefer to call things what they are." She shook a few into her palm and offered them to Simon. "Shriveled grape?"

"No thanks," he said.

"Your loss." She popped them into her mouth and chewed heartily.

An evening breeze drifted through the open window. The sound of little kids giggling came from one of the other apartments. Somewhere, someone was playing a cello. Unlike the front of the building, which was bustling, the courtyard side was peaceful. It was a sharp contrast to the person on his fire escape, who seemed more like a tornado in human form, who had continued to unpack a baggie of paper clips, a pewter triceratops, an empty package of potato chips, and a glow-in-the-dark souvenir key chain from Gingerbread Island.

"Here!" she announced, handing him a crisp business card.

AMAYA SHARMA

Pet sitting • Plant watering • Podcasting

Reasonable rates

No job too small (or big)

Her phone number and email were listed on the opposite side.

Despite himself, Simon was impressed. He'd never met someone his age with their own business card. He traced the raised letters with his finger. "You have your own podcast?"

Amaya chewed her bottom lip. "At first, I added it just because I wanted another "P" for my card. But then I thought I might as well. It seems like everyone has a podcast these days, and I *love* to talk, so . . ."

Simon was interested. He had a few podcasts that he liked and had wondered how hard it could really be to do the same thing. "What is it about?"

Amaya beamed. "I recorded my first episode with Professor Quintana and Ezekiel before the professor went on vacation to Peru. But I haven't edited it yet. Summer is a busy time for me. Besides Ezekiel, I'm watering plants for the Nguyens in 1A. Next week I'll take care of two hamsters in 3C."

A thought occurred to Simon. "Amaya? How did you know where to find me?"

She shrugged. "I overheard Oscar talking about the new family in 3B. This is the better of the smaller bedrooms because it has a view. It's the one I would pick, too. Plus, your light was on, so I'd figured I'd take a chance."

"Which apartment are you in?" Simon asked.

But before Amaya could answer, the peaceful night was pierced by a sound that was somewhere between a shriek and a beep. Simon heard it from inside the apartment, but—due to the open windows and the pleasant evening—the sound was amplified by the courtyard and echoed back up to Simon. The effect was earsplitting.

Amaya jumped to her feet. "It's a fire alarm!"

Simon spun in his chair, looking for his crutches.

Amaya paused. "Your parents are here to help you get downstairs?"

"I'm fine," Simon said.

He was about to ask if she wanted to come inside and join them in evacuating. But instead, she started climbing up the ladder.

Simon frowned. *Up* the ladder—not down.

He stuck his head out the window. "You're going the wrong way!"

"I've got to take care of something," she called. "I'll see you later, Simon. Nice to meet you!"

a speedy exit

"Sorry," Dad muttered. "Sorry, sorry."

He said it every time he accidentally jostled Simon's leg. Because the elevator was off limits during a fire alarm, they had to take the stairs. Which meant riding on Dad's back, aka the Piggyback Not-So-Express.

"It's okay," Simon said, even though on the inside, his brain was shouting, *Ow* and *Oof*.

Simon's heart thudded. He had been in fire drills before for school—but that was different. Fire drills had teachers and clipboards and kids messing around instead of paying attention. Apartment buildings didn't have fire *drills*. Did they? He'd never been in one. If there wasn't a smoke smell, it was probably okay. At least, that's what he told himself. But the truth was, his insides were flip-flopping on every step. He just wanted to be outside with Mom and Dad, away from the alarm and away from the chance of being trapped in a fire.

His parents had stayed true to their habit of traveling light—Dad carried Simon. Simon carried his rock collection. Mom carried everything else: her purse, two laptop bags, and a tote bag that included a folder with birth certificates and passports. It also held a thin blue photo album, which Mom insisted on carrying with her personally for each move, even though it had been backed up to the cloud in triplicate.

"Some things are too precious to be left behind," she was fond of saying. Simon was fond of rolling his eyes whenever she said it, even though a tiny part of him was glad that the album was important to her.

Some people weren't traveling so light. An older woman on the stairs ahead of them seemed to be struggling with a stack of boxes.

She turned to a person in a chef's uniform who wore eyeglasses with pink plastic frames. "Excuse me—can you give me a hand with this?"

"I'm sorry, no," muttered the chef, who broke away from the stairs and headed down the second-floor hall.

"I'll help," Mom offered and took the boxes from the woman, who beamed at her, brown eyes twinkling.

"Helen Kobayashi." The woman introduced herself with a slight Texas twang. "I picked up a bit more than I could handle."

They exited from the front doors. Residents crowded the steps.

"Clear the way!" said Oscar. "The fire department is going to need to get through here." He held a clipboard in one hand and his walkie-talkie in the other, which he waved about wildly.

"Is there an actual fire?" Simon asked.

Oscar glowered at him. "Alarms don't go off for no reason."

A mustachioed man in a lavender suit tapped his foot. "They certainly can go off for no reason—that's what a false alarm is. And that's what we have on our hands, isn't it? I can't abide this type of disruption. When will we be able to get back inside?"

"Can't you see I'm busy?" Oscar growled. "We won't know if the alarm is false until the firefighters can check out the entire building, and that's going to take a while."

The man sniffed, turned crisply on his heel, and marched down the stairs and away from the building.

Mom pointed at a planter with a wide ledge. Dad helped position Simon in a sitting position. Mrs. Kobayashi sat down, too.

"Thank you so much," Mrs. Kobayashi said as Mom placed the box at her feet. "When the alarm went off, I instinctively grabbed my files without fully appreciating how heavy they were."

Simon was curious as to why someone would take *papers*, of all things, if they thought their building might be on fire. "What's in them?"

Dad nudged him. "That's not exactly our business."

Mrs. Kobayashi smiled. "It's quite all right. Some of it is boring old paperwork. But I have case files in there, too."

Simon's eyes widened. "Are you a *detective?*"

Her eyes twinkled. Simon realized that she and Oscar were probably around the same age, but that was their only similarity. Her smile was gentle and sweet, but something told Simon that she wasn't a pushover.

"I'm retired now," she said. "My days of stakeouts and following clues are long behind me—I much prefer to spend my time in the courtyard garden or going to Zumba classes." She patted the box next to her. "But in some ways, it's not the kind of profession a person can truly leave. I've held on to all the materials for cases I was never able to solve."

A thousand questions sprang into his head—what was it like to be a detective? What did she mean that it was something a person couldn't leave? But his thoughts were interrupted by the fire truck screaming to a halt in front of the building. The firefighters unloaded efficiently, each with their own job to do. Their response was comforting—the exact opposite of the chaos unfolding on the street around them.

Oscar mopped his forehead with a dingy bandanna in an attempt to wipe off the sweat that glistened there. He gestured toward the building as he spoke to the fire captain. Meanwhile, a pair of firefighters placed a temporary barrier at the base of the stairs.

Some of the firefighters went inside the building. The others attempted to organize the crowd that was milling about.

Dad paced restlessly before announcing that he would go find out what he could about what was going on. Mom started talking to Mrs. Kobayashi about the Texas town she was from and how long she'd been living in Rigsby.

Simon shifted. His leg had begun to itch. He scratched the outside of his cast and studied his surroundings. Nearby, a man and a woman sat with a cat carrier between them. He had a long ponytail and wore a concert T-shirt, and she had short blue hair and hoop earrings. The man had several instrument cases next to him and held an electric guitar on his lap. It seemed that the two of them were having an argument.

"But we wouldn't have to worry about rent if you worked—" the woman said.

The man scoffed. "The drums are my job. They are my life!"

The woman folded her arms. "You get paid in *pizza*. The definition of a job is something that pays *money*. Actual dollars—on a regular basis," the woman answered sharply.

The man started to answer, but then he saw Simon watching. He whispered something to the woman, and they walked out of hearing distance.

Simon frowned. He looked around, wondering where Amaya was. Instead, he saw the chef, who sat next to an oversize box with holes poked into it. Occasionally, she peeked into the box, but Simon couldn't tell what was inside.

A woman wearing a backpack seemed to have her hands full with a few younger kids. A towheaded boy with a shark-tooth necklace, who Simon guessed was kindergarten age, kept trying to climb everything in sight: the railing, the ledge on the planter, a tree. A small girl with pale skin, pigtails, and sticky cheeks had her arms full of baby dolls. Nearby, a girl with light brown skin and dark, curly hair wore earbuds and practiced a soccer trick that involved balancing the ball on her knee.

"Fin," the woman said. "This isn't the time for climbing; please be patient." The boy nodded sweetly, but the second his mom turned away, he start climbing somewhere new, a mischievous glint in his eye.

The woman sighed, seeming to give up for the time being. "I'm Rebecca," she said to Simon and his parents. "Fin and Leah are my two—we live on the first floor. The soccer star is my niece, Hailey. She's eight years old and lives on the second floor with her dad."

She rummaged in her backpack. "I remembered to grab our important documents and my grandfather's silver watch. You'd think I could have grabbed some Goldfish crackers or applesauce packets, but no."

As Mom introduced herself, a small finger poked at Simon's arm.

Little Leah was looking at him with wide eyes. "Do you want to meet my babies?" She continued without waiting for an answer. "This is Ava, Ariana, Adrienne, and Albany. We have a stroller, but Mommy said we couldn't carry it with us." She sighed deeply at the injustice and then handed the dolls to Simon one by one. Some were more bedraggled than others—and one was actually an animal from that old show *Binkie Bunnies*—but it was clear that they were well loved.

"I guess names starting with 'A' are your favorite," Simon said, finally, to make conversation.

She scowled at him. "No." She pulled out a hairbrush and started brushing furiously at the swirl of hair on one of the baby's heads.

"Don't worry about her," Rebecca said over her shoulder, hurrying to remove Fin from a stair railing. "She takes her dolls very seriously."

After a while, Dad returned from the knot of people.

"It seems that someone pulled the fire alarm," he reported. "The most likely explanation is a prank, but they have to check it out thoroughly. We may be here a while."

"Delivery for Hyde!" A person wearing a bright-red collared shirt carried a big black bag through the crowd.

Mom waved him over. "Oh, thank goodness for pizza."

Luckily, Dad had ordered generously. After Simon took three slices of his favorite, pepperoni and green olive, Dad carried the boxes around to share with the other residents. He stopped to talk with Ginger, who stood a bit away from the crowd. Ginger was dressed more simply than before, having changed from her polka-dot dress into a shirt with umbrellas on it and white pants, her necklace now a simple silver chain. She didn't even carry a purse or any bags with her—the only thing she held was Bianca's leash. Bianca herself was in a little pink sweater that rolled above the edge of her bulging belly.

Time passed, and the majority of residents wandered away—from what Simon overheard, it seemed that they'd decided to wait it out at a café or restaurant. Most of the people with small children and pets stuck around—he saw dogs of every shape and size and several cat carriers. But that didn't explain what had happened to Amaya.

Simon yawned. Even though it was still early, the events of the day had tired him out.

"Attention," the fire captain spoke through her megaphone. "We have cleared the building and you all can reenter. The elevator is not available, but you can take the stairs to your residences."

Dad came back over. "Ready for the Piggyback Express? Next stop, apartment 3B."

With Mom's help, Simon clambered onto Dad's back. The group entering the building was in much better spirits on the way back inside—everyone was talking and laughing, relieved that there hadn't been a real fire.

But as they rounded the second floor, a scream rang out, echoing through the hallway.

"Help! Help! The Magnificent has been stolen!"

a cry in the night

Simon tightened his arms around Dad's shoulders.

"Come on—we have to help her!" he cried, even though Dad had already pivoted. Together they hurried down the hall, following the sound of sobbing.

The door to 2B was cracked as if it had been kicked in. Inside was utter chaos. The apartment had been ransacked. Drawers were dumped out, couch pillows were strewn across the floor, and even the artwork on the walls was askew.

Ginger paced the floor, walking in circles and sidestepping the clutter. She twisted a handkerchief she held in her hands. Tears flowed down her cheeks, and she made a wailing sound. Meanwhile, Bianca hunched in the corner, whining occasionally.

Mom went to Ginger. "Are you okay?"

The redheaded woman wailed. "I'm about as far as anyone could be from okay. The Magnificent—my ruby necklace—was right here when I left, but now it's gone!"

Simon's eyes widened. "Is anything else missing?"

Ginger shook her head. "They took only the necklace—but it's the most valuable thing I own. Plus, it's irreplaceable—an heirloom!"

"We probably shouldn't touch anything," Dad said. "I'm sure the police will want to take fingerprints. Did you call them yet?"

She shook her head and began to cry even harder.

"Okay," said Mom. "First things first. I'll call the police, and I'll wait with you until they arrive." She turned to Simon and Dad. "She's upset, understandably. You two go upstairs. I'll wait with her until the police arrive."

"But, Mom—" Simon started. He wanted to stay, to see what was going to happen.

Mom sighed. "No arguing, Simon. It's been an incredibly long day already. I'll be up as soon as I can."

When they got back to the apartment, Dad sighed deeply. He lowered Simon to a standing position and handed him his crutches. "That was not the way I thought we'd be spending our evening."

Simon nodded. "I wanted to eat our pizza sitting on the floor, like we always do when we get to a new place."

"We can do it another time," Dad offered. He rubbed his eyes. "I think I'll grab a shower. Are you thirsty?"

"I'll get it." Simon poured himself a glass of water and then headed to the couch, propping up his leg.

Moving days were always challenging, but this had to be the strangest one in Simon's entire life. He thought of Dad's expression when they saw Ginger's apartment—the concern in Mom's eyes as she told Dad and Simon to go on without her. Everything felt jumbled up and wrong. If only he could be downstairs with Mom, hearing all the details of the theft.

The timing of the break-in was awful. Plus, it seemed like Dad already had one foot out the door, dreaming of their next adventure. What if his parents made a big deal about this?

He heard a sound and reached for his crutches.

"Dad?" Simon asked tentatively. But all he heard was the rush of water from the shower. He settled back on the couch once more.

Then it started again. It was coming from his room, more insistent this time. The tapping sound.

Simon frowned. It had to be Amaya again. But what if it wasn't? A bolt of fear darted through him. He was being silly. Heart pounding, he went into his bedroom.

Amaya was at his window again, which was wide open. He'd left his room in a hurry when the alarm sounded.

57

"What happened to you?" Simon asked. "I thought I'd see you downstairs!"

"I had to grab Ezekiel," Amaya explained. "He hates commotion, so I found a quiet place to go—away from everyone else. I heard it was just a drill, but of course I didn't know that at the time—"

"Wait," Simon interrupted. "Did you hear what happened to the ruby necklace?"

She looked puzzled. "What necklace?"

Simon explained everything he knew about the Magnificent being stolen—which, unfortunately, was not very much at all.

After he finished, Amaya tapped her chin thoughtfully. "If it got stolen between the time of the alarm ringing out and Ginger going back to the apartment, that would be about ninety minutes."

Simon nodded. "I was wondering if someone saw her leave her place and just took the opportunity to grab it when the whole building would be gone."

Amaya squinted. "But how would anyone know she had it?"

"She wore it earlier today," Simon explained. "And it's a *huge* necklace—it's not something you could miss all that easily."

"Maybe this could be a good thing, in a way." Her eyes sparkled.

Simon frowned. "What do you mean?"

She twisted her hair. "It could be really good material for the podcast. A fire alarm being pulled, a burglary—that's not stuff that happens every day, at least not here at the Tangerine. Do you want to help? We could interview everyone and find out what they were doing when it happened. And if all the stories don't add up, we would find that out."

Simon hesitated. Amaya seemed like an interesting person—someone he might even like to have as a friend. But he was pretty sure this would fall into the category of stirring up trouble. He didn't want his parents to be focused on the burglary. In fact, he'd rather they forget about it as soon as possible.

"Simon?" Dad's voice came from the living room. "I made popcorn."

"Just a second, Dad!" Simon shouted over his shoulder.

Amaya rubbed her hands together excitedly. "We'll start interviewing people tomorrow. I'll make a list."

Simon hesitated. Code Name Chameleon, Part One was all about blending in. There was no way to do that if he and Amaya started knocking on doors.

"What time should I come by for you?" Amaya asked. "I was thinking of an early start. Maybe eight AM?"

"*No!*" Simon said. The word came out stronger than he meant it to. Amaya edged backward.

"Okay." She spoke slowly, stretching out the word. "How about nine, then?"

He cleared his throat. "Sorry. I meant to say that I don't think a podcast is a good idea."

Amaya looked hurt. "But . . . ," she began.

"Simon." Dad's voice carried from down the hall. "Do you want butter and salt or cinnamon and sugar?"

"I'm sorry. I have to go." He lowered the window and closed the curtains before Amaya could say another word.

After a few moments, he heard her footsteps on the metal fire-escape ladder.

It was his first day in Rigsby, and he'd already lost a friend.

a decision

Simon's dreams were full of rubies, star hair clips, green parrots, burglars, and fire escapes.

He was usually a good sleeper, but his brain was playing the argument with Amaya on repeat. He also kept thinking of the missing necklace. Ginger's apartment was right below his. The Hydes could have been a target just as easily as Ginger had been.

When Simon opened his eyes, he heard a tapping. *Amaya.* He pushed open the curtains, expecting to see her—but it was just a couple of pigeons.

He felt a pang but shook it off. It was just as well. He didn't want to get involved with Amaya's investigation. He picked up his crutches and opened his bedroom door. Dad sat at the kitchen table across from a tower of bagels. Mom stood, holding her phone at various angles to capture pictures of the food.

Mom was speaking in a low voice. "I just don't feel very good about it. On our first night here!"

Dad was about to respond when he noticed Simon. "Hello, sleepyhead. Are you hungry?"

Mom turned to smile at him, then gestured at the table. "Dad picked up breakfast."

Simon spread a thick layer of cream cheese on a sesame bagel. "What ended up happening last night?"

Mom twisted a lock of hair behind her ear. "The police came. Ginger was incredibly distraught."

Simon wiped his mouth. "That's really sad about her necklace. She said it belonged to her great-aunt or something."

Mom sighed. "It was a family heirloom. Irreplaceable."

Dad nodded. "It's also very valuable. Luckily, insurance will probably cover it."

Simon chewed thoughtfully. "How does that work?"

Mom put down her coffee. "So, let's say the necklace is worth a million dollars. You could take out a policy so if something happened to the necklace, you would be paid its value."

"I don't get it," Simon said. "How can the company afford to give everyone their money back?"

"Not everyone who takes out a policy will have their valuables stolen," Mom explained. "In fact, most of them won't. So you have to imagine lots and lots of people paying a smaller amount of money to get their policies, which covers the time when one of those people has a bigger loss."

"What if everyone *did* get their stuff stolen?"

Mom shook her head. "That would be unfortunate for the people—and for the insurance provider, because they would lose money. But I think those companies are pretty careful—they use math to figure out risk, and they're usually right."

"The whole thing is disturbing," Dad interjected. "Obviously, crime can happen anywhere. But in our building on the first night we arrived? In the apartment downstairs from us . . . it just seems like it's too close for comfort. What if it happens again?"

Mom reached over and squeezed his hand. "Of course it's unsettling. But the odds of it happening again are pretty low."

Dad sighed. "We could cut this lease short and move somewhere new before your school starts up. Maybe we should revisit that road trip idea."

Simon froze. "But we just got here."

Mom shot Dad a look. *"Thomas."*

Dad folded his napkin. "Okay, I'm sorry. I just worry."

Mom turned to Simon. "The best way to feel safe is to go out and make connections with your neighbors. It's true that we want a place where we can feel relatively secure with you walking around." She glanced at his crutches. "Well—when you're back to walking, that is."

He frowned. "But I *do* feel safe here. Last night was just a random thing. Plus, I already made a friend my age."

At this news, Mom beamed. "You did? Who?"

"The kid on the scooter yesterday—her name's Amaya. She has her own podcast. She is a pet sitter. And . . ." Simon trailed off, trying to think of another fact about her. "And she likes raisins."

Dad looked perplexed. "You can't stand raisins."

Simon sighed. "The point is, I don't want to move again—I want to stay here. For a while anyway—okay? Please?"

His parents exchanged glances.

"We'll be here for a while," Mom said firmly. Dad didn't look as convinced.

The bagel felt squooshy in his stomach. As much as Mom and Dad liked to say that they were all equal members of the family, the adults stuck together when it was time to make a decision. Rigsby would be the perfect fit if they would just give it a chance. He couldn't let a jewel thief derail his plan.

He pushed away his plate. "Wait. What if they solve the case?"

Dad sipped his coffee. "That would be a good thing."

Simon shook his head impatiently. "If the thief goes to jail, you won't have any reason to think about moving. Right?"

Mom nodded. "I suppose that's true."

Mrs. Kobayashi had been a detective. Maybe she would agree to investigate. "Is it okay if I go explore for a while?"

Dad raised an eyebrow. "On crutches?"

"Just in the building," Simon clarified.

"I don't know—" Dad started.

Mom reached over and touched his hand. "He won't go far," she said.

Dad nodded.

Mom turned to Simon. "Take your phone with you. Check in with us if you're going to be more than an hour."

Simon knew this was the most he could hope for at this point. He took a few big bites of bagel, then went back to his room.

He located Amaya's business card on top of his bookshelf. Her contact information listed only her cell phone and email—no address.

He typed her number into the messaging app.

> Amaya it's Simon
> Sorry about yesterday
> Where are you

Simon stared at the screen, waiting. Sending three texts in a row was a lot, especially for someone he didn't know well. But Amaya liked to talk and didn't seem to care about the regular rules people followed—like the general rule not to show up on someone's fire escape uninvited. So Simon's texts were probably okay. Unless she was mad at him for what he'd said last night.

Dots appeared to show that Amaya was typing back, but then they went away.

She was mad.

Simon shoved the phone in his pocket and shrugged on his backpack. He would have to find Amaya on his own.

CHAPTER 11

a search

If Simon could find Amaya, then he could explain everything. The problem was: he didn't know how to find her.

If he went to each apartment in the building, he would eventually find her. Sixteen apartments total minus the one he lived in meant fifteen doors to knock on. That seemed like a lot of walking around, especially when he was wearing a clunky cast. Besides, how would he explain that he was looking for a friend but he didn't know where she lived?

If only Oscar had been somewhat nice, Simon could just ask him. But he wanted to stay as far away from that guy as possible.

But then Simon remembered the basement. Maybe the mailboxes were labeled with all the last names of everyone in the building. He could check it out while he was collecting the mail for his family.

He said goodbye to his parents and headed for the elevator. While he was waiting for it to arrive, he pulled out his phone and opened the latest Hydes Go Seek post.

Swipe. A selfie of his parents grinning by the stack of boxes. That must have happened when Simon was downstairs with the van.

Swipe. A picture of light spilling into the conservatory, a close-up of some stained glass windows, a shot from above of the garden behind the building.

Swipe. A photo of the front of the Tangerine. *So much to love about our new home,* the caption read. *We can't wait to start exploring!* 😟 🚐 🏙️

But Simon couldn't help noticing that there was a lot the caption *didn't* say.

It didn't mention the fire alarm.

Not the tiniest hint about the Magnificent being stolen.

And of course, not a peep about possibly moving again—*already!*

There's an old saying: a picture is worth a thousand words. But you need more like ten thousand words to cover the real stuff. The messy stuff. The *true* stuff.

Recently, Mom had started asking permission before

posting pictures. So far he'd been saying "yes," but he was starting to think that he might start saying "no" sometimes, too. His parents tried to keep things real. But there was something about seeing the post that made the memory *less* real. It was like Simon could feel the actual experience being overwritten by the pretty picture and the caption.

Simon shoved the phone back into his pocket. The elevator arrived empty. Simon got on and pressed the "B" button.

In the basement, chain-link fencing created individual storage areas. Most seemed to have a bike or stacks of dusty boxes. One side had a laundry room, with rows of washers and dryers. In the corner was a door labeled OFFICE, which was probably Oscar's. Simon grimaced.

The mailboxes were in the center of the basement. Each metal door had its corresponding apartment number engraved on it. In addition, a few of the mailboxes sported name labels—some printed neatly, some handwritten. He stood on tiptoe to see the top row and leaned over to read the bottom row, until he had inspected each of them one by one. But Simon didn't see any that said SHARMA.

He took a step backward and almost tripped over a plastic tub half-filled with mail. Right on top were a few items addressed to 3B.

"*This* is what he was complaining about?" Simon muttered under his breath as he sorted through the coupons and advertisements.

The elevator doors chimed as they swung open and two people entered the basement. It was the couple Simon had noticed last night—the ones who had been arguing. They were getting along much better—they laughed together as they lugged overfull laundry baskets behind them.

Simon ducked down near the mailboxes, shoving great handfuls of papers and envelopes into his backpack as quickly as he could. Later, when he had time, he'd look through them and see if there were any good takeout coupons. Probably the whole mess would need to be recycled. It seemed like such a waste. He zipped the bag and slung it over his shoulders, then crept closer to the laundry room.

The man with the ponytail spoke excitedly to the blue-haired woman. He dropped his laundry basket and began to play air guitar. ". . . And then, the song'll go: *dun-dun-dun!* My heart is a renegade, *dun-dun-dun!*"

She was starry-eyed. "Oh, *Roger*. That. Sounds. Ah. *Mazing*." She had the way of speaking where every syllable sounded like its own word.

"I haven't figured out the *dun-dun-dun* parts yet,"

Roger explained. "But then it will go: *Before I met you, my life was a dead end. But now my love for you will never end.*"

Simon winced. Had Roger really rhymed "end" with "end"?

But Roger was just warming up. "Then the big finish: *Lois, oh Lois, it's yooooou that I miss!*"

The woman squealed. "Wait. *My* name. Is in. *Your song?*"

"You're my inspiration, baby," he answered. "I can only do my art because you believe in me."

Lois dropped her basket and jumped into his arms.

Simon rolled his eyes. They hadn't seemed to believe in each other last night, that was for sure. When they continued to the laundry room, he hurried onto the elevator. He couldn't stand listening to another second of their conversation.

Simon pressed the button for the lobby. He decided to head to the courtyard in the back of the building. On one side was a garden with raised beds. There were a few trees and a grassy lawn area with benches.

The little kids from last night were there, along with an older teenager on her phone. Leah, the littlest, was playing with her dolls. Hailey was reading a book. And Fin was perched in a tree. There was no sign of Amaya.

"Hi, Simon," Leah said seriously. "That's our babysitter,

Dolores." She pointed at the teenager. "I have my stroller today. See it?"

A crowd of baby dolls was crammed into a bright pink stroller.

Simon smiled at her. "That's nice. Is that—um . . ." He trailed off, trying to remember the names from yesterday. "Ava?"

Leah glowered at him. "No. This is Belle, Brielle, Bailey, Bella, Bibi, and Bubbles." She pointed at the dolls one by one in an authoritative manner.

Simon peered at the stroller. He wasn't an expert on dolls, but he was pretty sure that some of them had "A" names yesterday.

"Hey," he said, thinking of someone else with an "A" name. "Have any of you seen Amaya?"

Hailey and Fin shrugged. The babysitter said, "I don't know her."

Leah grabbed a baby from the stroller and squeezed it in her arms ferociously. "Amaya doesn't live here."

Simon was beginning to think that three-year-olds were a little intense.

"I *know* she doesn't live in the courtyard," Simon said patiently. "But I was wondering if you'd seen her."

"Hello!" a voice called out from the garden beds. It was Mrs. Kobayashi, kneeling by the tomato plants. "Simon, isn't it? Did I hear that you're looking for Amaya?"

Simon waved goodbye to Leah and the others and went over to the garden.

"Would you like a cherry tomato? This one is called Italian Ice." She handed him a small tomato that was a creamy yellow color.

Simon bit into it, and it burst on his tongue. He had expected a regular tomato taste, but this one was sugary sweet. "I didn't know tomatoes came in this color."

Mrs. Kobayashi smiled. "Oh, yes. You can grow purple, green, orange, and even black. Besides being delicious, they're very pretty in salads or salsas."

She showed him around the garden. There were all kinds of unusual vegetables growing—cucumbers that looked like lemons, white eggplant that looked like its color had been drained by Bunnicula, beans that were called "yard-long" but Mrs. Kobayashi insisted they were best if picked when they were twelve to eighteen inches long.

Simon looked around curiously. "This is not what I expected at all."

"I like growing unusual plants," Mrs. Kobayashi said. "It reminds me that things are not always what they seem."

"Is that something you learned from being a detective?"

"What I learned from being a detective could fill a

book," she answered, sighing. "But it's the type of work where there's always something new to learn. That's what I liked about it—that I was never done learning."

"Are you going to help find out what happened to the Magnificent?" Simon asked.

Mrs. Kobayashi shook her head. "I'm retired now and busy with my projects. Besides, it's much too close to home. That's a good way to get a lot of people mad at you—no one likes to be investigated, especially by one of their neighbors."

Simon could understand her point—which was a lot like the one he'd tried to make to Amaya last night. But after talking to Mom and Dad, everything had changed. If the thief wasn't found, his parents would make him move and he wouldn't have these neighbors anyway. Simon had nothing to lose.

A woman with ink-black hair entered the courtyard. Her hair was swirled into a messy bun. Under one arm, she carried a yoga mat.

"Hi, Veronica!" the kids called to her.

As Veronica waved at them, her gold bracelet glittered in the morning light. She gave the kids hugs and spent a long time admiring Leah's dolls in the stroller. Then she rolled out her mat and set up a wireless speaker that played calming music. When she started to do sun salutations, Fin and Hailey copied the best they could. Leah continued playing with her dolls.

Simon turned back to Mrs. Kobayashi. "Do you have advice for someone who wants to investigate?"

She took a long drink from her water bottle before answering. "Don't make assumptions. It's best to not have too many theories before you get started."

Simon leaned on his crutches. "Anything else?"

"Good detectives are people watchers. You need to think about why someone would be motivated to steal. Financial gain? Revenge? Was it planned or impulse? Who knew about the necklace?"

Simon frowned. "But how do you get people to talk to you?"

Mrs. Kobayashi's eyes twinkled. "People love to talk about themselves. All they need is an excuse. And, on the off chance you're talking about doing some investigating yourself . . ." Mrs. Kobayashi peered at Simon, who nodded to confirm what she was asking.

She smiled. "You have an advantage, because people won't be so on guard. People always underestimate kids, but I've found that they're some of the most observant people in the world."

Simon nodded. "That helps a lot," he said. "How can I thank you for your help?"

Mrs. Kobayashi looked thoughtful. "One more piece of advice: when in doubt, make cookies."

Simon laughed but added *Cookies for Mrs. Kobayashi* to his mental to-do list.

In his pocket, the phone buzzed. He pulled it out of his pocket.

> Meet me in the conservatory.
> Come alone.

CHAPTER 12

a plan

In the conservatory, Amaya had claimed one of the squashy armchairs. The green bird sat on her shoulder. She stared at him, her fingers steepled together.

Simon was struck with the sensation that she could read his mind and that she found it not up to her standards. He squirmed.

After a long pause, she spoke.

"Simon, Ezekiel. Ezekiel, Simon," Amaya said, by way of introduction. "Say hi, Ezekiel."

"Hi, Ezekiel!" the bird repeated. "Who's a good boy?"

Simon didn't know how to answer that one. "What kind of bird is he?"

"He's an Indian ring-necked parakeet. Sometimes they're called parrots, which is also correct. He's super smart and social and needs lots of attention, which is why Professor Quintana has me spend time with him."

He eased himself into the armchair next to Amaya. "I wasn't sure if you were mad at me."

Amaya raised her eyebrows. "You don't need to *wonder*. I definitely was. Am."

Simon's throat felt dry. Last night, she had wanted to convince him—but now, he wanted to convince her. "About the podcast? Because I've thought about it some more and—"

She held up a hand to interrupt him. "Because you didn't even *listen* to me. I don't care if you want to do the podcast, but you should pay attention to what I have to say. You closed the window on me!"

A flush creeped up the back of Simon's neck. "I'm sorry. I had to go because my dad was calling."

She raised her eyebrows. "Simon, I know it wasn't just because of that."

Simon's ears burned. "Fine. It was also because I didn't want to do it. But I changed my mind."

Amaya nodded decisively. "Okay."

"Okay?" Simon asked.

She tucked her legs under her, leaning forward as she spoke. "We can do the podcast. And we can be friends if you want. But that means we have to trust each other. We have to be a team. No lying. Is that a deal?"

He couldn't argue with that. "Do you think we can solve the case?"

As Amaya considered the idea, she tapped a pencil against her notebook, "If we're going through the trouble of interviewing everyone, we might as well try. First, let's make a timeline of everything you remember from last night."

Simon rubbed his temples, trying to think. On the way downstairs, they'd met Mrs. Kobayashi and the mysterious chef. Angry Oscar on the steps with his clipboard, and there was that man in the lavender suit. He'd seen the couple from the basement arguing—Roger and Lois, who were doing laundry in the basement.

As he spoke, Amaya recorded each name in the notebook. "Everyone is a suspect, unless we learn otherwise. And of course: Ginger. We have to talk to her."

"That's exactly where we'll start," Simon said.

CHAPTER 13

2B or not 2B

Two days later, Simon and Amaya stood in front of Ginger's apartment.

Of course, Amaya had wanted to begin immediately after they'd come up with the idea. But Simon didn't like to rush into things. He insisted that they wait and form a plan.

They had made a list of interview questions in a specific order. They had discussed how to ask her. First impressions mattered, and so did details. For example, when Amaya had showed him her tattered cardboard box of recording equipment, he'd been horrified.

"What's the problem, anyway?" Amaya had asked, strolling into his room like she owned the place.

Simon had grimaced. "We can't show up at her apartment carrying that dusty thing. Not only is it disgusting, she'll think we don't know what we're doing. We need to look professional."

Amaya's response had been a long sigh. She looked around the room briefly, then picked up Simon's backpack. "Can I use this?"

When he'd nodded, Amaya unzipped the backpack and dumped it out, gently nudging the pile of junk mail into his closet and shutting the door. "There. Happy now?"

"Much better," Simon had answered. The backpack was bulky with the heavy equipment inside it, but he managed it fine as they made their way to Ginger's apartment.

"Be friendly with her dog," Amaya had reminded him in the elevator.

"Of course," Simon had said. "Bianca is a great dog."

"Don't forget," she'd said as they approached the door. "Look around the apartment for clues."

Simon had sighed. "I already know that!"

Amaya balanced a plate of cookies in her arms now. Simon had mentioned Mrs. Kobayashi's advice, and Amaya had taken all of it seriously, down to the suggestion of cookies.

"Sorry," Amaya muttered under her breath. "I just want it to go well."

Simon looked at the door, which seemed to have been replaced or at least repainted.

Amaya knocked. Inside, Bianca barked. Eventually, footsteps approached. A series of metallic clicking and spinning sounds began, and Simon realized that several locks were being undone.

When Ginger peeked out, it was clear that she was still upset. Her hair was disheveled and her eyes seemed jumpy. Simon felt a pang of sympathy. It was probably really scary to have her apartment broken into, especially because it was just her and Bianca.

Ginger looked back and forth between them. "Simon and Amaya, right? Is there something I could help you with?"

As she spoke, Bianca trotted out of the apartment and sat at Simon's feet. He carefully leaned down to pet her—which was not easy to do while using crutches and wearing a heavy backpack—but it was worth it. She wiggled joyfully and rewarded him by licking the back of his hand.

Hello, we are working on a podcast so we can try to help solve the case of your missing necklace. Would it be okay with you if we came in for a while? We brought cookies.

This is what Amaya was supposed to say, according to the script she and Simon had worked on together. But what really came out was something like, "Hellopodcastnecklacecookies?"

Simon raised his eyebrows. He had thought that Amaya was the kind of person who never got nervous about anything, but apparently he'd been wrong. Ginger looked back and forth between them blankly. Amaya froze with a smile stuck on her face. Bianca flopped onto her side, displaying her impressive belly. Simon rubbed her ears. "We are working on a podcast and wanted to see if we could talk to you about the missing necklace."

"*Stolen* necklace," Ginger corrected him. "'Missing' makes it sound like it was lost, but it was taken from me. Ripped away by heartless thieves."

Simon nodded. "Sorry—stolen."

Ginger sighed, refastening a hair pin that had come out of place. "I think I have to say no. I've been a nervous wreck ever since it happened. I've already gone over all the details with the police, and I've been having nightmares. It would be upsetting to repeat that."

Amaya held out the plate. "We brought cookies." She seemed to have recovered from her attack of shyness.

Ginger seemed to think it over. "A podcast, you say? What is it about?"

"We're investigating the robbery," Amaya said. "And the necklace is the biggest news there's been for a while. We're going to do a few episodes where we talk to different people in the building to find out what they were doing the night of the theft."

Ginger tilted her head sideways. "If I say yes, will you let me know if you find anything in your investigation?"

Amaya hesitated, but Simon wasn't sure what the big deal was.

"Sure—we can keep you up-to-date," he said.

Ginger reached for the plate. "Well, I know Bianca would like to spend some time with you, Simon. Come on in."

When they stepped inside, he looked around the apartment. It had been tidied since the night of the burglary—all the sofa cushions were in place, and the books and knickknacks were back on the shelves. Ginger's decoration style was colorful, with lots of vintage items. Mom would have said it was *cute* or *darling*. A painting above the fireplace showed three redheaded girls and a gray cat sitting at the bank of a river. The girls' hair was long, and they wore old-fashioned-looking dresses.

Simon had been so shocked the night of the theft that he hadn't been able to take much in. But wow, Ginger had a lot of stuff. He couldn't imagine what it would be like to have so many things around all the time. So many connections to her past.

In the kitchen, Ginger filled a teakettle and put it on

the stove. She let Simon give Bianca a dog treat from the crystal jar on the counter—she gobbled it up like a high-powered vacuum. He patted her head, impressed.

Ginger placed a yellow polka-dotted teacup in front of each of them. She'd taken the time to move the cookies from Amaya's sturdy white plate to one with delicate flowers and a golden rim. Bianca had curled up by their feet.

Simon sipped his tea. It tasted like oranges and cinnamon.

"This is good," he said.

Ginger beamed. "You have excellent taste—it's considered the best tea in the world. It comes from Paris."

For just a second, Amaya froze in place. When Ginger turned back to the stove, Amaya pinched Simon's arm just above his elbow.

"Ow," he whispered, rubbing the sore spot. "What did you do that for?"

"I'll tell you later," Amaya muttered.

Ginger returned to the table, handing them each a pressed gingham napkin.

Amaya pasted on a wide smile. "Okay if I record?" She pushed the button after Ginger nodded. "First, can you introduce yourself?"

She nodded. "My name is Ginger and I've lived at the

Tangerine Pines for three years. It was my necklace that was stolen."

"Can you tell us about what happened that day?" Simon asked. When they were preparing, Amaya had explained that it was important to ask open-ended questions so Ginger didn't just say *yes* or *no*, which wouldn't be interesting on the podcast.

Ginger's forehead crinkled. "It was a typical Saturday. I went to the farmers market in the morning and then took Bianca for a short walk. That's where I met you and your parents on the steps. After we came back, I changed clothes. I was making dinner when the fire alarm went off. In all the hurry to get out the door, I must have forgotten to put the necklace in the safe. When I came back to the apartment, the necklace was gone."

Amaya's eyebrows drew together. "How did the thief get inside?"

"The police said the lock was picked," Ginger said. "There were all kinds of scratches on the lock—they said it was made by a long, thin metal object."

Amaya scribbled something in her notebook. "Can you tell us more about the necklace?"

Ginger touched the base of her neck, almost like she had forgotten that the necklace was missing. The corners of her mouth turned down. "As I told Simon before, it's a family heirloom. I'm the youngest of three sisters. Our great-aunt was one of those fabulous, elegant women who had many adventures. She was also very wealthy. She'd never married and was fond of her grandnieces. When she passed away, her will specified different items for each of us. For Clementine, a necklace of orange sapphires—very rare. For Olive, a necklace of brilliant emeralds. And for me, the Magnificent."

"Why is it called that?" Amaya asked.

Ginger dabbed her mouth with a floral napkin. "Like any work of art, jewelry is often named. It is a major piece—very valuable."

Amaya asked, "How valuable, exactly?"

Ginger shifted in her seat. "I happen to know exactly because I'd just had it appraised. I wanted to make sure it was fully covered by insurance. The necklace is valued at one million dollars."

Simon's mouth dropped open. Amaya looked just as shocked as he felt. He'd had no idea how much it was worth.

"For a *necklace*? Just one necklace, right?" Amaya asked, as if she couldn't believe it, either.

"Just the one," Ginger said grimly.

They were quiet for a moment as that information sank in.

Ginger cleared her throat. "I wanted to ask you two if you'd seen anything suspicious that evening."

Simon scrunched his forehead, thinking. "When we were out on the steps?"

Ginger nodded, nibbling her cookie. "Then . . . or even after that. Specifically—this may be a bit strange, but did you happen to see anyone that night or the next morning in the basement?"

Amaya looked puzzled. "The basement? But that's not anywhere near your apartment."

Ginger dusted some crumbs off the tablecloth. "It's just a thought—you know, that they might have seen something."

Simon shrugged. "I saw the musician and his girlfriend doing laundry there. Roger and Lois? Maybe they saw something."

Suddenly, Amaya leaped to her feet. "Is it okay if I record some ambient sounds? You know—the background kind of noises that a podcast plays to establish a scene. Like chickens clucking whenever someone goes to a rural town. It's always chickens for some reason."

Ginger looked startled. "I don't have any chickens."

Amaya crossed the room, stopping at the fireplace mantel. "It can be anything. Refrigerators humming, birds singing, clocks ticking—like this one."

She made a recording and then disappeared down the hallway.

Simon chewed his cookie, looking out the window at the modern-looking apartment building next door. His phone buzzed.

> Keep her busy for a while

"Everything okay?" Ginger asked.

Simon shifted in his seat. "Um, yes. So that building next door. It sure is big."

He winced inside at the awkwardness of his words, but Ginger didn't seem to notice. She glared out the window.

"It dominates the entire view. It's such an eyesore," Ginger said.

Simon didn't think the building was *that* bad—but if he said that, Ginger would stop talking.

"I guess I don't know what it looked like before," Simon said.

Ginger sighed. "I used to have a view of Piney Park. I'd drink my tea every morning and look out at the trees and all the joggers and children playing. And now I see glass and steel. I wish they'd tear it down."

Ginger walked to the sink and began to rinse an empty plate. "Is your family settling in okay?"

Simon took another cookie. "Overall, we're doing okay, I think. Mom and Dad are worried about the break-in, though. That's part of why I wanted to help investigate—I don't want them to worry about it happening again."

"Do you have siblings, Simon?" she asked.

Simon shook his head and braced himself. As far as he could tell, the worst part of being an only child was listening to other people's opinions on it. Most of the time, they weren't positive. He'd been told he'd never learn how to share without a sibling, which was absolutely ridiculous. He was very good at sharing. He'd also been told that only children were always lonely. Simon sometimes was lonely, but it had much more to do with the fact that his family moved so much. He didn't think that would be solved if his parents had chosen to add another kid or two to the family.

Ginger smiled. "You're very, very lucky. I wish I'd been an only child."

Simon paused. On the one hand, it was refreshing to have someone say something positive about being an only child. On the other hand, it was a little unusual for an adult to talk about wishing their siblings didn't exist.

She laughed. "The look on your face! I just mean that older siblings can be very bossy. They always think they know what's best, even when they definitely don't. And sometimes the youngest gets left out of things—intentionally or not."

Simon didn't have time to ask for more details because that was the moment that Amaya returned to the kitchen. She raised her eyes at Simon in an I've-got-a-secret kind of way. Moving quickly and efficiently, she stashed the recording equipment in Simon's backpack and then turned to Ginger.

"I think that's all we need for now," Amaya said. "If there's anything else, is it okay if we come back later?"

Ginger dried her hands on a polka-dotted tea towel. "Of course—anytime."

Ginger and Bianca walked them out. When the door was about to close, Amaya said, "Sorry, just one question. I know you mentioned you were wearing the necklace earlier that day. Do they think someone might have followed you back from the farmers market? Maybe you were targeted by a thief."

Ginger shook her head. "I wondered the same thing. But Oscar kept a record of everyone who exited the building for the fire alarm. There weren't any strangers or guests on that list."

Simon frowned. "What about the back door? Could someone have exited that way?"

"Impossible," Amaya answered. "Remember, Oscar was painting the floor in the back of the building. The paint was still wet, and the building doors were sealed off."

Ginger nodded. "With the timing of when the theft occurred, it had to be someone who lives in the building. The thief is someone who lives in the Tangerine Pines." She shut the door gently.

Simon's stomach flip-flopped. The theft wasn't random; it was targeted. And the thief was someone who lived right there in the building. If Mom and Dad knew, he'd be packing boxes faster than Bianca could scarf down a dog biscuit. He looked at Amaya. They were going to have to solve this case—fast. But how?

suspicious minds

Simon and Amaya got in the elevator. As soon as the doors were closed, Amaya turned to him.

"Now that," she said dramatically, "was *weird*."

Simon leaned against the railing. "What do you mean by that?"

Amaya tapped the plate she was carrying. "Did you notice that she had to move the cookies from my normal dish to a fancy one? Don't you think that's unusual? And don't even get me started on the dog treats in the crystal jar."

Simon shook his head. "I don't think that's such a big deal."

Amaya frowned. "Then she said that the tea was from *Paris*—no way. That was the regular grocery-store kind."

"Is that why you pinched me?" Simon sighed. "Maybe she likes things to seem fancy. That's not exactly a crime."

"It's not," Amaya admitted. "But it's strange. And I haven't even shown you what I found in the hall when I was making my recordings."

The elevator doors chimed. Simon and Amaya got out on the third floor. As she walked, Amaya pulled up a picture on her phone. She handed it to Simon.

He squinted at the screen, which showed a framed black-and-white photograph of three buildings. "I have no idea what I'm looking at."

Amaya sighed, zoomed in on the building in the middle. "You really don't recognize it?"

Simon tilted the screen back toward him. Something *did* look familiar—the brick walls, the arched windows, the double front doors.

"That's not the Tangerine Pines, is it?"

Amaya's eyes were wide and excited. "It's an old photo—taken before the building on the left was torn down."

Once again, Simon found himself staring at a picture, trying to understand the bigger story it told. This photograph was like looking back in time. The trees that lined the street were there but much smaller. A person walking by wore an old-fashioned-looking suit and a hat.

Simon shrugged. "Maybe she likes history."

Amaya switched off the phone. "One thing is for sure—we need Oscar's list of all the people who were in the building. We have to go talk to him."

His stomach sank. "No thanks. I'm staying as far away from Oscar as I can."

Amaya rolled her eyes. "You have to come with me—we're a team. Besides, he's not that bad."

Simon looked at her sideways. "He basically said I was inviting crime into the building by propping the door open for, like, three minutes when I was standing right there."

Amaya slipped the phone back into her bag. "We need that list, though—we'll have to figure that out tomorrow."

They stood in front of Simon's apartment.

"Do you want to come in?" Simon asked.

"Better not," Amaya said. "First, I need to take care of Ezekiel, and then I have piano, and then I'm doing something for my mom. Tomorrow we can start working on the podcast. Maybe we'll also find Oscar and find out about that list."

Simon paused. "You don't always have to come over here, you know. I could go to your apartment sometime. Which one is it?"

Amaya twisted her green hair. "My apartment? No,

it's okay—you have a broken leg! I'll come to you. See you tomorrow."

She waved goodbye and hurried down the hall.

Simon opened the door to 3B. Inside, Dad was sitting at the kitchen table with his laptop.

Dad nodded toward the office. "Mom's just finishing a call. Then we thought we'd try the ABC Pancake Diner around the corner. Did you know that they're open all day long and they have twenty-six different kinds of pancakes on their menu? Should we go there for dinner?"

Simon grinned. There had been many questions since he'd moved to the Tangerine Pines, but this was the one that had the easiest answer. Pancakes were always a good idea.

a mission

The next morning, it rained steadily. After breakfast, Simon was straightening his room when he heard a tapping at the window.

Of course, it was Amaya, soaking wet. He unlatched the window for her and scooted backward, rolling over the creaky floorboard that made its *krr-squeak* sound.

"I have news for you," Simon said as she climbed inside. "There's a little invention called a front door. Regular people knock at them."

Amaya grimaced, kicking off her sneakers. "Whatever gave you the idea that I would want to be a *regular person?*"

She tossed her hat on top of her shoes, which were already creating a sizable puddle on the wood floor.

Small silver stars dangled from her ears, and her jeans had rips at the knees.

Simon snorted. "Right. Why would anyone want that?"

She raised an eyebrow. "Oh, be quiet. I know you aren't a regular person, even if you try to act like one."

Simon sat in his swivel chair. "Who would you say *is* a regular person, though?"

Amaya didn't hesitate. "Calvin Morris—he's still on vacation or you probably would have met him already. Smart, popular, athletic. Everyone likes him except me."

"That doesn't sound so bad," Simon said.

Amaya made talking motions with her hand like she was holding a puppet. "Blah, blah, blah."

Before Simon could respond, she spotted his bookshelf and crouched down to examine it.

"You can learn a lot about a person by their books," Amaya said, star earrings swinging. "I don't mean just the titles—I mean the *way* they read them." She removed a well-worn copy of one of the Tristan Strong novels from the shelf and began to flip through it.

"This is a perfect example. Missing dust jacket. Dog-eared pages. Looks like you like to snack while you read." She pointed at a page with a dusty orange fingerprint, then held it to her nose. She sniffed deeply. "Cheese puffs?"

Simon's cheeks reddened. "Yeah."

Amaya slammed the book shut. "Don't be embarrassed. If it were a *library* book, I would definitely judge you. You have to be gentle with library books or any that belong to other people. But something from your own shelf? You have a right to read exactly the way you want to."

Simon opened his mouth to speak, but it seemed that Amaya was just getting started. She sat on the floor with her legs crisscrossed, her arms gesturing wildly.

"The way I see it is this: if you're reading a really good story and you can't put it down, isn't that the biggest compliment an author could ever get? When I have a book I love, it's with me constantly. That means I have it when I'm eating my breakfast and brushing my teeth and even"—she paused for dramatic effect, eyebrows arching—"when I'm on *public transportation*. It goes with me in my school bag and to the park and the beach. So what if it gets a little rained on or a little smooshed at times? If you can still read the words, then everything is fine. If you ask me, the only people you shouldn't trust are those with shelves and shelves full of books that look like they've never been touched."

Simon nodded. "One time we went to an open house and they had glued all the pages of the books together. They were just for decoration."

Amaya shuddered. "Horrifying."

She carefully put the book back on the shelf and turned back to Simon. "Let's start working on the podcast."

This was, unfortunately, easier said than done. The problem was that Amaya and Simon had very different ideas of what the podcast should be like. Amaya leaned toward making the story as dramatic as possible, with sound effects like sirens and fire alarms and a woman screaming. Simon was more concerned with representing the facts in a calm—Amaya would say *boring*—manner.

Simon sighed. "Maybe we should finish investigating before we start doing the podcast."

Amaya's forehead wrinkled. "That's not how the big podcasts do it."

"They have their own production staffs—and interns and things like that," Simon said. "I think we should focus on the detective part first."

She frowned. "Is that just because you want to find the thief so you can prove to your parents that it's okay to stay here?"

Simon bit his lip. Amaya had a way of being direct that was unlike anyone he'd ever met. But she'd already told him how important honesty was to her, so he figured he'd better tell the truth.

He cleared his throat. "Maybe. But I also think that it's hard to tell the whole story as it's developing. For example, it would be a very different podcast if they end up catching the thief tomorrow. Or if they never solve it. It can be hard to tell the story when you're right in the middle of living it."

Amaya seemed to think it over. "I see what you mean. Also, if we can focus on investigating, maybe we'll actually be a part of solving it. And I did think about something new after we talked to Ginger."

Simon raised his eyebrows. "Well? What is it?"

She straightened her ponytail. "Oscar's list—if he really did write down everyone's name as they left, that means that the thief is someone who evacuated the building after Ginger did. Because that's when the necklace was stolen, right? Sometime between when she left her apartment and when she returned."

Simon's eyes widened. He nodded. "I wonder if the police know that."

Amaya scrambled to her feet and handed Simon his crutches.

"We don't need the police," she said. "We need Oscar to give us a copy of that list."

It took longer than usual for the elevator to arrive. Finally, the doors opened. Fin and Leah were inside with their babysitter, Dolores. The children wore rain slickers and yellow boots. A plastic sheet covered the doll stroller. Amaya pressed the "B" button for the basement level.

Leah pulled at Simon's arm. "We're taking my babies outside for a walk. Dolores said we could have one elevator ride before we went out so we went all the way up to the tippy-top floor."

"I'm going to splash in lots of puddles," Fin announced, stomping his feet on the floor.

"Where's Hailey today?" Simon asked.

Fin's lower lip stuck out. "Soccer camp."

They got off at the first floor and waved goodbye to Simon and Amaya.

When the elevator doors closed again, she turned toward him. "Let me do the talking."

Simon was happy to agree to this. The fewer interactions he had with Oscar, the better.

The elevator doors opened, and Simon and Amaya exited into the basement. They approached Oscar's office, which was tucked into a corner of the laundry room. Several loads whirred away, spinning in the dryers.

As they got closer, they heard Oscar's unmistakable voice.

"No, no, no," he said grumpily. "Something bigger." Amaya flattened herself against the wall outside the office. She held her fingers to her lips to signal to Simon that he should be quiet.

There was a pause. Was someone in the office with Oscar, or was he on the phone?

"How much are we talking?" Oscar asked.

There was another pause. He must be on the phone.

"Listen," Oscar continued. "You aren't the only game in town, you know. I can always go elsewhere for what I need—"

A loud buzzing sound echoed through the room. Simon was so startled that he jumped—forgetting that jumping with a broken leg was almost impossible. He stumbled. Horrified, he watched in what seemed like slow motion as one of his metal crutches fell to the ground with a clatter.

Amaya spun to look at him, scowling. "It was just the dryer!" she muttered under her breath.

She bent down to retrieve the crutch and handed it to Simon. When they looked up, Oscar's large figure loomed in the doorway. In one hand, he held a phone. In the other, he held a wrench.

Oscar held the phone to his ear. "I'm going to have to call you back." He pressed a button to end the call. With a few squeaky steps, Oscar was in the doorway, glowering at them.

Simon gulped.

Oscar narrowed his eyes. "Can I help you two with something?"

The words weren't sinister, but there was something in his tone that made Simon cringe.

Luckily, Amaya did not seem anywhere near as disturbed as Simon.

She beamed a brilliant smile in his direction. "Hi, Oscar!"

He folded his arms, forehead glistening with sweat. "Amaya . . . *Simon.*"

Simon flushed. He had never known someone to squeeze so much disdain into the two syllables of his name.

Amaya tucked a piece of hair behind her ear. "We wanted to ask you about the missing necklace. I heard you were helping with the investigation."

He shifted uncomfortably. "It's a terrible thing."

She nodded. "Ginger said you even kept track of all the people who evacuated the building."

Oscar removed the bandanna from his pocket and wiped at his forehead. "Well. It was the least I could do."

"That was super smart," Amaya said sweetly.

Wow, she was really laying it on thick. Simon started to roll his eyes, but he realized that Oscar was looking right at him.

Simon tried to pretend he was fascinated with the ceiling, but quickly realized that was even more awkward. He pasted a smile on his face and glanced at Oscar, who continued to stare at him suspiciously.

"The thing is," Amaya said, "Simon and I are trying to help. We were hoping we could see that list?"

Oscar's jaw tightened. "Our residents value privacy. Sharing the information with the authorities is one thing. Giving access to a couple of kids? I don't think anyone would take kindly to that."

The walkie-talkie squealed, and Oscar spoke into it. "Yes, okay, I'll be there in a few minutes."

He returned to his office and sat in his desk chair. Simon and Amaya stood at the doorway. It looked like he had been in the middle of a meal—a half-eaten breakfast and a cup of coffee rested on top of a stack of files. The room was cluttered with papers and boxes on almost every surface. A pegboard on the wall displayed various tools. The outlines had been painted around them, so it was easy to tell at a glance what was there and what was not.

Simon shot a glance at Amaya, who looked at him blankly.

He cleared his throat. "Looks like you're missing a hammer and a pry bar."

Oscar narrowed his eyes. "If you must know, they're being used on a job site. I used the pry bar to take off moldings when I was painting."

"And the hammer?"

"To put the moldings back on," Oscar said shortly. "Look, I can tell you kids are trying to help, but it seems like this is best left to the authorities."

Amaya tapped her fingers together. "But isn't it in the best interest of the building that the theft gets solved quickly? Simon and I won't get in anyone's way—we're just trying to collect the information and help solve the crime."

The walkie-talkie squawked again. Oscar sighed deeply and then took a sip from his coffee. "You want to help, huh?"

Amaya nodded so fast, Simon thought she might get whiplash.

Oscar studied them. "What exactly is it worth to you?"

Simon raised his eyebrows. "What do you mean?"

Oscar leaned back in his chair. "There's one thing I hate about my job. If you can help me with it, I'll help you get your hands on that list."

Simon and Amaya exchanged glances. What could be the worst part of Oscar's job? Collecting rent? Fixing toilets? Dealing with trash or dog poop or bugs?

"Anything," Amaya said.

Simon frowned. He wouldn't go *that* far. He definitely wouldn't do anything involving heights.

Oscar's mouth curved in what could only be described as a smile. He got to his feet.

"Paperwork," he said, pointing at his desk. "If you file everything, I'll make sure to leave a copy of the list where you can find it. Got it?"

Amaya clapped her hands. "It's a deal!"

a mountain of paperwork

"I think my eyes might be permanently crossed," Simon complained, pushing himself backward in the desk chair.

Even with his blurry vision, he could see Amaya's scowl from where she stood at the filing cabinets. "You think that's bad? I have, literally, three thousand paper cuts."

"You don't *literally* have three thousand paper cuts," Simon objected. "If you literally had three thousand paper cuts, you would have almost no skin left."

Amaya wiggled her fingers. "That's exactly what it feels like. Pretty soon you'll be able to see my skeleton."

He sighed, looking around the room. Tools hung from hooks alongside duct tape and a coil of scratchy rope.

There was a bulletin board of notices. And, of course, Oscar's pile of papers—which was much smaller than it had been a few hours ago. The filing system was straightforward, but the sheer quantity of pages meant that progress was slow.

Simon tilted his head back, looking at the ceiling. He slowly spun himself in circles. His mood was sour. Between the dim light and the tiny print on the invoices, he was getting a headache.

He cleared his throat. "I think we got the worst side of this deal by a lot. We should have found out exactly how much filing we had to do first. But no, you had to act like filing was the most exciting thing that had ever been invented."

Amaya ignored him. She was frowning at a piece of paper.

"Don't you think so?" Simon asked. "Hello, Amaya, are you there?"

She continued to stare at the paper.

Simon wheeled his chair over to her. "Did you find the list?"

"What?" Amaya looked up, her eyes wide. "No. It's something else."

She held the paper so Simon could see. It was a list of names, numbers, and dates.

He scratched his head. "I don't get it. Why is that important?"

"It's a record of the rent payments, organized by unit. See where it says 3B—Janice and Leah Washington? They lived in your apartment before you did. They had a little dog named Freddy who I would walk sometimes."

"Okay," Simon said, not really seeing the point. "And?"

Amaya tapped the page. "All the residents are listed by last name except one."

Simon squinted. "Who?"

Amaya tapped the line where 2B was shown. "This is Ginger's apartment, but it doesn't show her name. Instead, it just says 'Three Pines.' That seems so familiar—have you heard of it before?"

Simon shrugged. "Maybe it just sounds familiar because of the name of the apartment building. Why are there so many things having to do with Pines? There's Piney Park down the block, and the building is called the Tangerine Pines. There aren't even any pine trees around here."

Amaya raised her eyebrows. "The building was named after the owner—her name was Tangerine Pines. You know that painting in the conservatory? That's her."

Simon imagined the face of the old, red-haired woman from the painting. She'd been holding a dog—or was it a cat?

"I've never met anyone named Tangerine," Simon said.

Amaya shrugged. "There're a million names in the world. It makes sense that you wouldn't have heard of some of them."

She had a point.

Simon scooted his chair back to the desk and sorted the remaining papers into piles. He pushed one paper too far to the edge of the desk, and it fell off, fluttering into the wastebasket.

"Oh no," Simon muttered. He leaned over the trash can and fished out the paper. But there was something else that caught his eye—a crumpled envelope that said,

READ ME.

He held it up to show Amaya. "There's something inside. Should we look at it?"

Amaya rolled her eyes. "Obviously—it even says 'read me'!"

He removed a piece of paper from the envelope and smoothed its wrinkled surface.

CONSERVATORY
TOMORROW
9 P.M.
I NEED TO TALK TO YOU.

His stomach sank. He couldn't believe what he was reading. Did this prove that Oscar was the thief?

Amaya elbowed Simon. "Amazing! We *have* to be there."

Simon frowned. "There's no date. Do you think it's tomorrow, or some date that already happened?"

Amaya studied the paper. "It was right on top, wasn't it? It's at least worth a try."

Simon gulped. "I don't know. Maybe we should give this to the police."

She scoffed. "No way! There's nothing *illegal* about a note saying for someone to be somewhere. Besides, Oscar could just say he found it when he was sweeping. It doesn't even have his name on it."

Simon knew she was right. They were going to have to show up in the conservatory to see for themselves.

Ding!

The elevator chimed, and the doors slid open.

"Simon!" Amaya hissed. "Put the paper back!"

Hands shaking, he refolded the paper and placed it in the envelope.

Squeak. Squeak. Squeak.

"That's Oscar's shoes," Amaya whispered. "He's coming now. Hurry."

Her voice was so calm that it was somehow worse than if she had screamed at him. Simon's heart was pounding like a drum. He shoved the envelope back into the trash can and tried to arrange his face into a normal expression.

Oscar stuck his head into the room. "All finished?"

Simon nodded stiffly.

Amaya's eyes twinkled. "You have good timing. Can we see the list now?"

She sounded exactly like her regular self. Inwardly, Simon admired this. Outwardly, he felt like he was going to throw up. He swallowed hard.

The corner of Oscar's mouth turned up in a half smile. He stepped inside the room, removed a page from the bulletin board, and handed it to Amaya.

Simon groaned inwardly. The paper had been in plain sight the whole time. They could have saved themselves a lot of time—and a *lot* of filing—if they'd thought to check the walls. But then again, if they'd spotted the list right away, they would have missed the envelope's mysterious message.

Amaya snapped a picture with her phone and then

handed the paper back to Oscar. Simon grabbed his crutches and followed her out the door.

"Thanks again," she said.

Oscar glowered. "Don't mention it—to anyone."

a question of motive

"Let's see that list," Simon said.

Amaya's gaze darted around the basement as if she were triple-checking that they were alone; then she pulled up the photo on her phone and held it so they could both see.

Rebecca—Fin, Leah, Hailey
Ginger
Lorenzo
Roger and Lois
Helen K.
Hyde
Jordan
Veronica

"He has messy writing," Simon complained.

Amaya elbowed him. "He wrote it in the middle of a building evacuation. I'm sure neatness wasn't high on his list of priorities."

He zoomed in to examine the names. "Your family's not on the list."

"My parents were out. I must have evacuated Ezekiel before Oscar started writing names."

He frowned. "What if the thief did the same thing?"

Amaya shook her head. "That wouldn't make sense. When Ginger left her apartment, the necklace was still there. It would have to be someone after her name."

He sighed. "The idea is that it's one of the people who left the building after Ginger did—that someone broke in after she left her apartment."

Amaya nodded. "Who on the list seems most suspicious to you?"

Simon pointed to the two names he didn't recognize. "Who are Lorenzo and Jordan?"

Amaya tapped the names. "Lorenzo is the man in the lavender suit. Jordan is the chef. There's something weird about Jordan if you ask me. I think she has something to hide. Once, I gave her my business card for pet sitting, and she looked at me like I'd handed her a snot-encrusted tissue. She walked away without saying a word."

Simon chewed his lip, thinking. He wasn't sure that it was all that suspicious. Amaya could be a little overwhelming. Probably she'd given Jordan a bonus, long-winded speech to go along with that card.

He snapped his fingers. "I remember Lorenzo. He was *really* mad about being delayed to get back inside the building."

Amaya scrunched her nose. "The necklace had already been stolen at that point. Wouldn't the thief be more likely to try to blend in as much as possible?"

"Maybe," Simon allowed. "Or maybe he wanted to get back in the building so he could hide it in his apartment."

They were quiet for a moment. It was unsettling to think that someone could have been holding the necklace the whole time they were outside on the steps. Maybe it was even someone they'd shared their pizza with.

"What else do you remember about that night?" Amaya asked.

He scrunched up his forehead, remembering. "We met Mrs. Kobayashi on the way downstairs. She had some heavy boxes, but Jordan wouldn't help because she had something else to do."

"*See,*" Amaya interjected. "She has something to hide. I told you!"

"We should look at the list and see who we can eliminate. Then we can focus on the suspects."

Amaya looked unsure. "I don't think we can rule out anyone at this point."

He frowned. "It's definitely not you or me. Or our parents. So who do you think it is—sweet old Mrs. Kobayashi?"

Amaya tightened her ponytail. "Maybe we should ask ourselves who would have wanted it."

He sighed. "It was a million-dollar necklace. It would be easier to make a list of who *wouldn't* want it."

Amaya shook her head. "Our best lead is that envelope we found. Tomorrow night in the conservatory. Do you think it's about the necklace?"

Simon narrowed his eyes. "I don't know—but tomorrow night we're going to find out."

a new friend

That evening, Simon and his parents walked around the corner to the ABC Pancake Diner, which had immediately become their favorite neighborhood restaurant.

It wasn't *just* a pancake restaurant, even though they were definitely the highlight. There was a huge doughnut case with wild flavors like Lime-Marshmallow and Super Strawberry Sprinkle Surprise. Simon breathed in the smell of maple syrup, sausage, and piping hot pancakes. The diner was another place that gave him that forever kind of feeling. It had a blue-and-white-checkerboard floor and blue vinyl booths. On the walls were murals of breakfast foods doing different activities—it was the kind of mural you could look at every day for a year and always find something new. Their menus were organized to look like a children's ABC book. Each page had full-color illustrations of a different pancake. Simon had decided to work through the menu in order, which began with Apple Dumpling and ended with Zebra Stripe. That night, he ordered the Triple B: blueberry, banana, and buttermilk.

After they put in their orders, Mom told a funny story about her conference call that afternoon. Then she turned to Simon. "What were you up to today?"

Simon made trails in the condensation on his water glass. "I was with Amaya. We're making a podcast."

Dad raised his eyebrows. "What's it going to be about?"

Simon made a face. "We're supposed to be investigating what happened to the Magnificent. But we spent most of the day organizing Oscar's office."

Mom laughed. "That's very nice of you—but what docs it have to do with the missing necklace?"

He paused. Simon didn't want to lie to his parents, but Oscar had said they shouldn't mention the list to anyone.

"We were just trying to get more information about what happened," Simon answered. "We're planning to interview people who were there that night and see if there are any clues the police may have missed."

Mom and Dad exchanged looks.

"Simon—are you sure that's a good idea? Getting involved in the investigation, I mean," Dad said. "The simple fact is that there is a burglar who was in our apartment building. As long as you are with a friend, I don't mind you exploring the building. But if you're asking people questions about the theft, I'm a little concerned."

Simon bit his lip. Mom and Dad didn't know that the list of suspects had been narrowed down to people in their building. What would they say if they knew he and Amaya were planning to go to the conservatory the next night to see who Oscar was meeting?

He needed a new approach. "But, Dad—you both said you'd feel a lot happier here if the crime gets solved. I love Rigsby—I don't want us to move just because of some necklace."

Dad sighed. "I hear that you don't want to move right away. But Mom and I have to make the decision that's right for the family."

"I'm part of the family, too," Simon said. "And I want to stay."

Before Dad could reply, their server appeared at the table, arms stacked full of plates. He gave Simon his Triple B pancakes, then put the Key Lime pancakes in front of Mom and the Yuzu-Yogurt in front of Dad. Before they could eat, Mom wanted to snap some pictures. Simon could imagine the post.

Swipe. Here we are at the ABC Pancake Diner, ready to eat the alphabet!

Swipe. It's so fun to have adventures together as a family—especially delicious ones! Yum, these pancakes are amazing!

Swipe. There was a crime in our building! So much so that we are considering moving—except Simon doesn't want to anymore.

Just kidding—that last one would never happen.

He scooted sideways in his chair so he wouldn't be in the picture. Mom moved the pancakes around until she had all the photos she wanted. Finally, they could eat. They were quiet for a while as they dug into the golden, lacy stacks that were just crisp on the outside and airy and fluffy within.

After a few moments, Mom reached over and squeezed Simon's hand. "We aren't making any plans to leave. We just want to make sure we're in a safe place."

"Hi there, neighbors," a quiet voice murmured.

Simon looked sideways to see a woman with yellow eyeglasses. Instead of the chef's uniform, she wore a plain white shirt and a backward baseball cap.

"Jordan, what a nice surprise!" Mom said. "I don't

know if you've officially met my husband and son." She introduced Dad and Simon, and the chef gave each of them a tiny wave.

"Jordan and I met the other day when we were both heading out for a run," Mom explained. "I didn't realize you worked here."

Jordan straightened her apron. "I usually work at Mariposa Kitchen downtown—but the owners of this place are old friends, and I fill in when they're short-handed. How are your pancakes?"

While his parents raved about their meals, Simon peered at Jordan. She *seemed* nice enough—but why would she refuse to help nice Mrs. Kobayashi? Maybe Amaya was right to be suspicious of her.

He swallowed a buttery blueberry-banana bite. "I remember you from the night of the fire alarm. Mrs. Kobayashi asked you to help with her boxes, but you wouldn't. Why not?"

Jordan flushed.

"Simon!" Dad said. "Watch your manners."

Jordan straightened her ballcap. "I was worried about my pet ferrets. I'd loaned someone their carrier and needed a way to get them safely downstairs. I should have found a way to help her, Simon—but I'm glad your family stepped in."

Her story, technically, made sense—but Simon couldn't shake the feeling that something seemed off. He remembered Amaya saying that Jordan didn't want to talk about pet sitting with her.

"I like ferrets—could I meet them sometime?" Simon asked. "How many do you have?"

Jordan glanced around before answering. "The building has a limit on pets—two is the maximum. And no, they're very shy and don't like visitors—I'm sorry." She glanced at her watch and said she had to get back to work, then hurried to the kitchen.

"She seemed very nice," Dad said.

Simon hesitated. "*Sort* of. She rushed off when I asked about her ferrets."

Dad swallowed a bite. "Remember, Jordan is working. She had to get back to make the food."

She did make good pancakes, Simon had to admit.

"She was very nice when she was telling me about the jogging paths," Mom said. "I'm happy to find another runner in the building."

Simon looked at Mom, who was smiling widely. Unlike Dad, she didn't make friends easily. He could talk to strangers on a train, in a plane, even in a grocery line, and within minutes, he'd know their whole life story. Mom and Simon took a little longer to find their people. Maybe Jordan would be Mom's new friend.

"These pancakes are extraordinary," Dad said. "And bonus: now we've met a ferret-owning pancake chef. That's the great thing about moving—always meeting new people and experiencing new things."

Simon chewed quietly. He didn't fully trust Jordan, even if it was hard to say exactly why. In theory, the best way to be safe was to get to know the people around him. But maybe that was different when one of those people was a thief.

After dinner, Simon and his parents walked home. It was a warm summer evening with a light breeze—one of those nights where everyone seemed just a little bit happier than usual. The sky was streaked with purple, and the street was bustling. Someone on the corner was playing the saxophone, and Dad dropped some money in the case.

Mom tilted her head at the little grocery store. "We need fruit and almond milk. I'm going to run in for a few things."

Dad and Simon decided to wait on a nearby bench. A crowd of bicyclists whirred past. They moved in perfect synchronization, like they were part of the same multi-headed, many-wheeled being.

Somehow, the city felt alive—kind of like a friend. But

it was hard to enjoy that feeling when the threat of moving away hung over Simon's head. If he and Amaya solved the case, they'd stay . . . for a little while. But it would only be a matter of time before his parents suggested moving, and Simon's life would be in boxes—again.

Dad patted his belly. "I think I ate too much. But those pancakes are so good, it's hard to stop."

But Simon didn't want to talk about food. "Can I ask you something? Why do we move around so much?"

Dad scrunched his forehead. "You know why—it's what the Hyde family does. We're always looking for something extraordinary. It can be hard to find that if you stay in the same place your whole life."

Simon waved his hand. "I've heard you and Mom say that, but I feel like that isn't the main reason. When Mom was a girl, she lived in three different houses, which I think is a medium amount of moving. But you lived in the same town—the same house—until you left for college."

Dad tapped his chin, thinking. "There's such a big world out there," he said finally. "When I was a kid, I felt bored in the town I lived in. I never wanted you to feel that way. Mom and I are lucky enough to have jobs where we aren't stuck in one place. Don't you like seeing new things?"

"I do," Simon answered. "But I think I would like living in the same place for a while, too. Coming back to school at the same place for a second year. Not having to be the new kid all the time. I think that would be an adventure, too, in a way."

Dad made a noncommittal sound.

Out of the corner of his eye, Simon spotted a streak of green across the street. It was Amaya on her scooter, darting by. Ezekiel clung to her shoulder, screeching delightedly.

"Pretty baby! Here's a kiss—mwah, mwah!" the parrot shouted.

Simon raised his hand, about to call to them—but then something curious happened. Instead of riding by the mansion, Amaya cut her wheels to the right. She coasted by the lush topiaries and followed the path up to the front door. The uniformed man smiled and said something to her as he held open the door. In a fluid motion, she picked up the scooter and went inside, Ezekiel still on her shoulder.

Dad looked at Simon questioningly. "Isn't that Amaya? I thought she lived in our building."

Simon nodded. Yes, Amaya definitely lived in their building. But why would she be going to the big house next door?

"You mentioned that she pet sits," Dad says. "She probably has a job there."

"That must be it," Simon said. But it was strange that she'd never mentioned it.

Dad rubbed his chin. "I wonder what kind of pets they have in that big old house. They could probably fit a herd of elephants inside and no one would ever know. Good thing Amaya's a professional."

Simon shook his head as if to clear it. Amaya had probably dropped off a business card there and gotten the job that way. It was impressive, really, the way Amaya knew how to take charge. She was the most confident person he'd ever known.

Mom came out of the store carrying two big bags. A bouquet of hydrangeas—Mom's favorite—peeked out of the top of one.

Dad got to his feet, grinning. "Seems like you got a few things besides milk."

Mom laughed. "It's such a cute store! And they had my favorite flowers—how could I say no to that? They'll look great in pictures for The Hydes Go Seek."

When they returned to the apartment building, a few adults were standing outside chatting. There weren't so many people on this part of the street—it was mostly neighbors from the Tangerine Pines. Mom and Dad sat on the steps, chatting with Mrs. Kobayashi.

A small hand grabbed at his arm. "Hi, Simon!" Leah's hair was in pigtails, and she wore a shirt with a fox on it. She pointed at her doll stroller. "See my babies? I dressed them very fancy tonight because they are going to a ball."

At that moment, the last thing in the world Simon cared about was dolls, but he didn't want to hurt her feelings. He nodded. "That's nice."

Her brother, Fin, swung from a nearby tree. He was wearing his shark-tooth necklace. "Simon doesn't want to play with babies. He wants to watch me climb. See? See how high I am?"

"Yeah," Simon said vaguely. He began to wonder how much longer his parents would be.

Something flew by his ear with a *whoosh*. Simon turned his head to see a Black boy around his age. He was about Simon's height, with a wide smile and a fade haircut with a design line.

He held up a Frisbee. "Sorry about that. My brother is just learning to throw. Malik, be more careful!"

He launched the disc, which arced perfectly toward a younger boy, Malik.

Malik caught the disc and then smiled widely, pumping his fist. "I got it, Calvin!"

So this was Calvin—Amaya's archenemy. He didn't seem very enemy-ish.

Between throws, Calvin introduced himself. "Mr. Oscar told us a new family moved in while we were on vacation. We're on the fourth floor. Are you Simon?"

Simon nodded, but before he could say anything more, Calvin was hurrying to catch the disc again. He jumped, snatching the disc from midair.

"Nice catch," Simon said.

"I think it's getting too dark to see," Calvin called to his brother. Malik shrugged and began to climb the tree with Fin.

Calvin jogged back to where Simon was standing, spinning the Frisbee on his index finger.

"Earlier this summer, I did an ultimate camp," he said. "It's kind of a mix between basketball, football, and rugby. But instead of a ball, you use the Frisbee. It's no-contact and there are no referees. I pretty much love every sport, but I *really* love ultimate. We can play if you want, after your leg is better."

Code Name Chameleon automatically popped into Simon's mind. But for the first time, something made him hesitate. After all, he hadn't used Code Name Chameleon on Amaya, and that had gone okay—better than okay. Amaya didn't seem like the kind of person who would change for the sake of someone else. That was one of the best parts of Amaya, actually.

Simon grinned. "I'd like that."

They said goodbye, and Simon joined his parents on the steps. For the first time in ages, he wasn't thinking about blending in or being weird. It seemed like spending so much time with Amaya had changed him a bit. She didn't care at all what other people thought of her. The Tangerine Pines had so many different people—and everyone seemed to belong. Maybe he didn't need Code Name Chameleon anymore.

"Ready to head inside?" Mom asked.

Dad held the door for them, and they went inside. Simon knew it probably wasn't their forever home—knew they wouldn't have one while Dad still thought that something extraordinary was around the next corner. But just for that night, Simon allowed himself to hope that this was a forever kind of place.

lists, laundry, likes, and lies

The next morning, Simon woke up thinking about how he would explain leaving the apartment that night. His parents were already a little worried about him because of his leg. Now, with the stolen necklace, they seemed like they were even more on edge. Leaving at night might be a bit tricky. He would have to come up with a plan.

He walked into the kitchen and poured himself a bowl of cereal.

Mom looked up from her laptop. "Good morning. Did you see how many likes we got yesterday?"

Simon leaned against the counter. "I didn't notice."

Mom grinned, stretching her arms over her head. "People are loving our move to Rigsby. I'm working on a few top-five lists—places to eat, to shop, to people watch."

Simon chewed thoughtfully. Mom worked hard on The Hydes Go Seek, and he was glad that people liked it. But at the same time, he knew that likes could come and go. He wanted a stable foundation to build on. Once, he saw a tree that toppled during a rainstorm, its underside a scraggly tangle. Dad had pointed out that the root system was shallow—no match for the wind and the soft, water-soaked earth. Simon wanted his family to dig in deep.

He swallowed a spoonful of cereal. "You like *other* things about Rigsby, though . . . not just the content you and Dad can make from it. You actually like the ABC Diner and our building and our neighbors and everything. Right?"

"Of course," Mom said distractedly, pecking at the keyboard.

"And you think it's important to have those things in a place you live. Right?"

"Uh-huh," Mom answered. She was so absorbed in her work that she sounded light-years away.

Simon took another bite of cereal. "Mom, tonight Amaya and I are going to go spy on Oscar. Okay?"

Mom peered at the screen. "Mm-hmm."

"We think he might be a vampire alien who is part of an international jewelry smuggling ring," Simon couldn't resist adding.

"All right," Mom muttered, resizing an image.

Simon sighed. "I'm going to take out the trash and recycling."

At this, she finally glanced up. "You'd have to go all the way downstairs. Are you *sure* you can manage?"

As he balanced on his good leg, Simon hefted the bag in one hand, looping the drawstrings over his wrist. "I can do it—it's not even that heavy."

Mom hesitated, but then her computer made a *ding* sound, and she went back to what she was doing. Before she could stop him, he'd swung the bags over his shoulder and gone out the door, heading for the elevator.

In the basement, Simon emptied the bags. But just as he closed the dumpster lid, he heard a sound from the laundry room. He peeked around the corner and saw Ginger. She knelt on top of one of the machines, attempting to peer behind it. When she saw Simon, she gasped, holding a hand to her chest.

"You startled me!"

Simon looked apologetic. "Did you lose something? I could try to reach—or maybe Oscar could help."

"Yes—no!" Ginger said, sounding flustered. He waited for her to explain, but she was quiet.

He didn't think he had surprised her *that* much—but it was clear she was on edge. She seemed so different from the first day he'd met her. Back then, she'd had a vintage dress, her hair was perfectly styled, and she had worn the Magnificent, of course. But in the laundry room, she wore baggy gray sweats and a shirt that was so old, it seemed to be no color at all. Underneath her freckles, her skin was pale, highlighting the deep purple rings under her eyes. Her previously shiny red hair was flat and frizzy. It looked like she hadn't slept in weeks.

Ginger took a deep breath, tucking a piece of hair behind her ear. "I mean—*yes*, I lost something. And *no*, I don't need Oscar. That's the last thing I need." She muttered the last part under her breath and went back to looking behind the machine.

Simon paused. He didn't know Ginger well, but he was concerned about her. Maybe there was something he could say to put her mind at ease. Simon still wasn't sure that he completely trusted Oscar, but Amaya did—and she seemed to know this building and its residents well. If Ginger went to Oscar, he might help her find whatever she was missing, and then she'd have one less thing to be worried about.

"I didn't start off right with Oscar," Simon said. "But the other day, he helped us. Of course, we had to help him first by doing all his filing."

Ginger's eyebrows arched sky-high. "He let you into his office? He usually won't let anyone in there."

He grimaced. "We were there for *hours*. I have the papercuts to prove it."

Ginger's face brightened. She hopped down from the washing machine, looking at him carefully. "You said he helped you. Did you find a clue?"

"We found two things," he said.

Her eyes widened. "Go on."

"First was a mysterious letter asking Oscar to meet in the conservatory at nine PM."

"Interesting," she said, stretching the word out. "What are you going to do about that?"

"Amaya and I are going to show up and watch him," Simon said. After he blurted out the words, he was worried that Ginger would tell him not to—or worse, that she would tell his parents. But instead, she just nodded.

"I think that's a very good idea," she said. "What was the other clue?"

Simon leaned on his crutches. "Oscar made up a list of all the people who left the building."

Her eyes turned down in a disappointed way. "I already knew about the list."

Simon didn't want her to be discouraged. "Amaya figured out that the *order* of the list was important. It had to be someone who exited after you did."

Ginger took a step closer to him. "Very interesting. Do you have it with you, by any chance?"

He patted his pocket. "I have it on my phone. But . . ."

Ginger's eyes narrowed ever so slightly. "But *what*? No one wants to find the Magnificent more than I do. I told you that it's a family heirloom. I told you all about it for your little podcast. I'd really like to see the list. Please."

Simon hesitated. He'd promised Oscar and Amaya to keep the list a secret. But that meant from the building in general. It had to be okay for Ginger to know. She was the one who'd been stolen *from*.

He put the password into his phone and pulled up the image of the list, which Amaya had texted him. Ginger studied the image carefully, like she was trying to commit the names to memory.

"Oh, I'm being silly," she said. "Do you mind if I forward this to myself?"

Before Simon could say anything, she tapped the screen a few times, and the swoosh sound played that meant a message had been sent. She handed the phone back to him.

"There—done. I don't know if it will help, but it's a much shorter list than it was before," she said.

Simon's mouth felt dry. "Oscar said we shouldn't show anyone. I probably should have said that before."

Ginger sighed. "He's weirdly secretive. He's started locking his office when he's away from it. What could he be hiding in there?"

Simon shook his head. "I have no idea."

She patted his arm. "You made the right decision. It will be our little secret."

Ginger waved goodbye, leaving the laundry room looking much more cheerful than she had before. That had to be a good thing, didn't it?

That evening, when Simon asked to go downstairs after dinner, he expected his parents to argue.

But instead, they thought it was a good idea. Maybe *too* good of an idea.

"We'll keep you company!" Dad said. "I've been wanting to explore the conservatory and see what kinds of books they have."

Simon's eyes widened. "No, that's okay. I'm meeting Amaya."

Mom patted Dad's arm. "Simon wants to be able to hang out with his friend. He doesn't want us to tag along."

Dad widened his eyes, pointing at his chest dramatically. "Do you not think I'm cool enough? Me? I'll have you know, I was once *very* cool."

Simon winced.

Mom grinned. "I think the operative word is 'was.'"

Dad laughed. "All right, all right. It feels a little late, but I guess you're getting older. Stay in the building. Be back by nine thirty."

Simon beamed, heading out the door before Dad could change his mind. Once outside, he breathed a sigh of relief. He took the elevator downstairs and went through the lobby. No one was in the conservatory. He checked the time on his phone. It wasn't like Amaya to be late.

"Pssst!"

Simon looked around but didn't see anyone. He was sure that Amaya had said to meet him here. He took out his phone to text her but was interrupted by a creaking sound.

He turned toward the noise. The wall was *moving*. No, that wasn't quite right. It was a panel near one of the bookcases. And it was swinging open.

Amaya's face appeared, grinning. "Greetings and salutations."

Simon stared at her. He couldn't believe what he was seeing. "I was trying to text you! Did you just come out of an actual wall?"

Amaya stepped backward. "Come on in—there's plenty of room. Turn your phone to silent."

He peered inside. It wasn't just a wall—it was a small room. There was an ancient mop and a few stacked boxes. Everything was dusty, which made Simon think that the room was not being actively used. The fretwork design on the panel disguised the fact that parts of the wall were made of screening. Someone inside the room would be perfectly hidden—but still able to hear and see everything happening in the conservatory.

"It's called a service room," Amaya said. "Old fancy houses were built with them. Even when this one got converted into apartments, they left some of these passageways and secret storage areas."

Simon frowned, puzzled. "Why would a house need a secret room?"

"Super-rich people owned these places," Amaya explained. "When they were having fancy dinners, they didn't necessarily want their servers lingering around while they were talking about important things. But the servers needed a way to find out if people were ready for the next course or if they needed more water—that kind of thing."

Simon craned his neck to see the secret room better. "So they'd just wait there and listen in? Like spying?"

Amaya tapped the intricate fretwork on the outside of the wall. "See these wood designs? There's a mesh screen behind them. So the servers could wait here and see and hear what was happening but not be in the way of the fancy people."

She showed him how it worked. The room was accessed by a groove to one side of the panel. On the inside of the room was a latch that, when pushed, made the door swing open.

Simon was impressed. "How did you find it?"

Amaya tugged at her earlobe. "The house next door has the same thing."

He was about to ask her how she had discovered *that* when he heard it.

Squeak. Squeak. Squeak.

Amaya grabbed his arm. "It's him! Get inside!"

She pushed Simon into the room and closed the door.

When Oscar came into view, he was not wearing his usual coveralls. Instead, he wore a sweater vest and a blue bow tie. He rubbed his hands together and glanced around the room.

Light from the conservatory filtered into the room where Simon and Amaya stood. She looked at him quizzically. "What is he wearing?" she mouthed.

Simon shrugged.

Oscar picked a few pieces of lint off the purple velvet

sofa. Then he examined the bookshelves for a very long time. Just as Simon thought Oscar had fallen asleep standing up, he selected a volume and eased himself into a squashy armchair. But even as he turned the pages, he spent more time gazing around the room than he did looking at his book. Every time the elevator chimed, he straightened his shoulders and seemed to ready himself. But the people getting off the elevator—first Fin and Leah's mom and later Lorenzo, clad head to toe in lavender—never once glanced in the direction of the conservatory.

Simon slipped his phone from his pocket and checked the time. He held it up for Amaya.

"What should I do?" he whispered. "I have to be back home in twelve minutes."

"Just hang on a bit longer," Amaya muttered. "We can't exactly pop out of this panel and say, *Good evening.* I think we'd scare him to death."

Simon shifted impatiently. The seconds ticked by.

Oscar looked at his own watch and sighed deeply. Groaning, he got to his feet. He adjusted the angle of the armchair and plumped a pillow on the sofa. Then Oscar walked out of sight, his shoes *squeak-squeak-squeak*ing the entire way.

"I don't know what that was," Amaya whispered.

"Me neither." Simon's fingers found the latch, and he was about to swing the panel wide when Amaya pinched him just above the elbow.

Voices echoed in the lobby. After a few moments, Roger the musician and his girlfriend, Lois, entered the conservatory. They flopped on the velvet sofa. The pillow that Oscar had so carefully tidied fell to the floor in a slump.

Lois crossed her arms tightly. "Absolutely unreliable."

Roger groaned. "It isn't my fault that he didn't show."

She poked him in the side. "It's not *not* your fault, either."

He sighed, covering his eyes. "Just believe in me. That's all I ask."

Amaya leaned over to Simon. "Are you thinking what I'm thinking?" she whispered.

Lois sat up straight. "What was that?"

Roger looked around, blinking sleepily. "What was *what?*"

Lois swiveled her head from side to side. "I swear I just heard a voice."

Simon and Amaya stared at each other, eyes wide. She'd overheard them. Amaya clamped her hand over her mouth, as if she were afraid a sound might escape of its own will.

Roger scratched his head, yawning widely. "Probably a weird echo. You know these old buildings."

Lois didn't look convinced.

"That reminds me," Roger said. "I was thinking we should add an echo effect on the chorus to 'Baby I Got a Fever.' Don't you think that would make it more haunting?"

They launched into a long discussion about whether Roger's idea was a mark of genius (Roger's opinion) or just a gimmick (Lois's opinion). The conversation went on for so long, Simon's arms fell asleep from holding his crutches.

After what seemed like ages, they finally stood up and moved toward the elevator.

Simon slowly counted to fifty and then reached for the panel. "Let's get out of here."

He held the door for Amaya, who exited quickly and fastened the latch behind her.

"Do you think they were planning to meet Oscar? Why did they come in right after he left?" Simon asked.

Amaya shook her head slowly. "I don't know what to think—but I do know that they just moved up a few spaces on our list."

CHAPTER 20

another mystery

"You did *what?*"

Simon buried his face in his hands. "I know, I know. I'm sorry!"

Amaya scowled at him from the other side of the elevator. They were heading to 1C in an attempt to catch Roger and Lois at their apartment. That morning, Amaya took Ezekiel out for a stroll, and they'd bumped into Lois. When Amaya explained the podcast, she had waved her arm vaguely and said they were usually home in the afternoons.

"Oscar said not to show anyone else," Amaya said. "The last I heard, the definition of 'anyone' definitely includes Ginger."

Simon shifted, leaning against the wall. "She just

looked really sad. She wants her necklace back more than anyone."

Amaya narrowed her eyes. "What did you say she was doing there anyway—laundry?"

He sighed. "She didn't have a basket, and the machines weren't running. I think she'd lost something behind one of the machines. Maybe something she put on top of the machine fell backward or something."

Amaya frowned. "I don't trust Ginger."

"Why? She's on our side," Simon said.

Amaya seemed not to hear him. "She's hiding something—I'm sure of it."

Simon sighed. "You just don't like her because of the tea from Paris."

"But it *wasn't* from Paris," Amaya said. "That was the whole point. I can't stand it when people aren't honest."

Simon rolled his eyes. "Fine. But she doesn't have to tell us everything about her life just because we're interviewing her for a podcast."

"You're right," Amaya said. "It's not like she's a *friend*. A friend who said he wouldn't share information with anyone else. A friend who *promised*!"

Simon groaned. "I said I was sorry about that. She took me by surprise. I won't tell anyone else about the list."

The elevator doors opened on the first floor. Calvin and Malik were waiting to get on.

Calvin grinned. "Hey, Simon. Hey, Amaya." Malik lifted his hand in a wave, his smile showing that he'd lost one of his front teeth.

Amaya swooped past them, not saying a word.

Simon's jaw dropped. He knew she didn't like Calvin, but that was pretty rude. He shrugged apologetically, holding the elevator door so the boys could get on. Before the doors closed, he leaned forward. "Calvin? Do you think you could show me a few throws sometime? I know it might not be very fun when I'm on crutches, but I could try."

Calvin's smile got bigger. "Yeah, definitely. I'll stop by sometime."

After the elevator doors closed, Simon caught up to Amaya, who was standing in front of Roger and Lois's door. Her arms were folded tightly.

"What was that all about?"

Amaya's eyebrows drew together. "I told you that I don't like him."

"You might if you gave him a chance," Simon said.

Amaya scowled. "He's a friend stealer. He moved here a few years ago, and everyone immediately wanted to be his best buddy. It's totally unfair."

Before Simon could reply, Amaya reached out and rang the bell. She pressed hard enough that it seemed like she was making a point.

"Remember," she whispered, "look around for anything unusual. Are they having money problems? Do they seem like they might have taken the necklace so they could sell it?"

After a few moments, Roger came to the door. He wore a shirt with a hedgehog on it, and his eyes seemed sleepy.

He looked back and forth between them for a moment, seeming confused. Then he slapped himself on the forehead. "Right, right. You're the ones with the podcast. Lois! Those kids are here." He shouted the last part over his shoulder, then held the door open so Simon and Amaya could come in.

The living room was tidy and simple. Concert posters hung on the wall, and a fish tank glowed in the corner. A bookshelf held an extensive collection of vinyl records. Roger plopped on a lime-green corduroy couch and indicated that Simon and Amaya should sit in the mismatched chairs on the other side of a scratched coffee table. He picked up a guitar and plucked at it.

Simon lowered himself into a floral armchair. It was old but surprisingly comfortable. A black cat with green eyes came over and sniffed his cast.

"That's Ink Blot. We call him Inky for short," Roger said.

"Cute," Amaya said. "I'll leave you one of my cards in case you ever need a pet sitter."

Roger continued to strum on the guitar.

Amaya pulled their equipment out of Simon's backpack. "Okay if we record?"

Roger flipped his hair out of his eyes. "Of course. I'm a professional."

"You're in a band, right?" Simon asked. He figured it was good to get Roger talking about something he liked.

From the kitchen, Lois scoffed. "A band that spends more time arguing than rehearsing."

Roger sighed deeply, continuing to play.

Lois entered the room, carrying a large bowl of chips. Simon thought she would offer some to everybody, but instead she sat cross-legged on the floor next to the sofa, balancing the dish on her lap.

She crunched a large mouthful before speaking. "So you're trying to figure out what happened to that necklace?"

Roger stopped strumming. "Wait. I thought this was about my band, Angry Hedgehog."

Lois sighed. "I *told* you that it was about the break-in."

Roger snapped his fingers. "We should tell them about what happened last night."

Amaya and Simon exchanged glances.

"What happened?" Amaya asked.

Roger leaned forward. "Someone broke into our apartment!"

Simon's mouth dropped open.

Amaya's eyes shone. "Tell us everything."

"Well," said Lois, chomping on another handful of chips. "We aren't *totally* sure."

Roger tapped the side of his guitar impatiently. "I worked a late shift at the ABC Pancake Diner—I just started there as a waiter. Lois came to meet me at the end of my shift so we could eat together because—hey, free food. Then we went to my band practice, but no one showed up. When we got home, our lock was all scratched up. That's a sure sign of someone trying to pick it."

Amaya made a note, then looked around encouragingly. "Then what happened? What was taken?"

Roger paused, his shoulders slumping.

"See, that's just it," Lois said. "Nothing is missing. I mean . . . *nothing.*"

"That we know of," Roger added.

Lois shook her head. "But the weird thing is, we can tell that some things got moved around. The sweaters in my dresser were folded differently—I know that sounds weird, but I have this special way of rolling them so they take up less space. But this morning when I opened the drawer, they were all folded flat."

"Also, my vinyl collection." Roger pointed at the bookshelf with the records. "Some of the albums are in a different order. Why would that happen?"

Simon turned to Amaya, raising his eyebrow. It didn't seem exactly like concrete evidence. How reliable were Roger and Lois?

"And you're *sure* nothing was taken?" he asked.

"Positive," Lois said.

"I don't know," Roger said. "If there was, we haven't been able to figure out what it is. I even had a big stack of cash on my nightstand from my tips at the diner. They didn't even take that."

"That is really weird," Amaya said. "I wonder what they were looking for."

"Maybe they broke in for a different reason," Simon said—even though he couldn't imagine what that would be.

Lois looked skeptical. "What would the odds be of two different burglaries happening around the same time, in the same building?"

The thought of two different people breaking into apartments was too much for Simon. But he didn't have to worry about what to say next. Because somehow, no matter where the conversation was heading, Roger managed to steer it back to the topic of Angry Hedgehog. So far, Simon had learned that the band practiced every day, except when there was a full moon. They played a variety of instruments, including the piccolo. And Roger described their style as disco-folk-punk, with a splash of emo. Unfortunately, he had played them several songs to show exactly what he meant by that.

Simon's ears were starting to feel tired.

Luckily, Lois interrupted. "Don't you have a shift in a little bit?"

Roger glanced at his watch, sighing. Simon glanced at Amaya. It seemed that it was time to go.

Amaya had that look on her face that said she wouldn't be distracted. "Why did you start working at the diner?"

Roger scratched his head. "On the night of the fire alarm, we went there to wait. We've been a bit short on cash, so Lois, uh, *suggested* that I fill out an application. I've been working there ever since."

Simon thought back on the night of the alarm, when he had spotted Roger and Lois for the first time. He remembered them arguing about money. Inky was at his feet again, rubbing his face against Simon's cast. That was it.

"You had Inky with you when you went to the pancake diner?" Simon asked.

Roger smiled. "We had to sneak him in, but that was easy to do with all my instrument cases."

Lois looked up at him, laughing. "So many instrument cases!"

He squeezed her shoulder. "When there's a fire, you realize what's the most important of all. Music, Lois, Inky. That's all I need."

Gross. While Roger and Lois gave each other sappy looks, Amaya scribbled something in her notebook. Then she carefully tilted her head sideways so only Simon could see; then she crossed her eyes and stuck out her tongue.

Amaya stood up. "I think that's all we need. Thanks for letting us come over."

Simon followed her to the door. They waved a final goodbye and shut the door behind them. He leaned against the wall, thinking.

Amaya turned to him. "I guess we can cross Roger and Lois off the suspect list. They were fighting about money, and then he got a job. That's why they were so happy when you saw them in the laundry room the next day. And they're ultra-lovey-dovey now that they know what's important." She rolled her eyes so hard that Simon half expected them to fall out of her head.

"It still doesn't explain why they were in the conservatory last night," Simon said.

"Maybe it was a coincidence. At least their cat was cute."

That made Simon remember something. "Why did

you ask about whether Inky was with them during the fire?"

Amaya looked thoughtful. "I thought it would be a good way to see what's really important to them. Only the thief knew it wasn't a real fire. So it seems like people would be hurrying. They only had time to take a few of their most important things, right?"

Simon nodded, thinking of his parents' documents, cameras, laptops—and of course, his rock collection, which had all made the cut.

Amaya pointed at some marks on the lock. "Here are the scratches that Roger mentioned."

He squinted at the door. "Who do you think would have the kind of tool to pick a lock?"

Simon's and Amaya's eyes met.

Simon snapped his fingers. "Oscar! It has to be him."

Amaya shook her head. "He has keys to all these apartments! He could literally just walk in if he wanted to." She sighed. "I don't know that I really trust Roger and Lois. Don't they seem kind of . . . forgetful? Or like they may have imagined their things being rearranged?"

"It does sound strange," Simon agreed. "It would be a lot of trouble to break into someone's apartment just to move some things around."

"Exactly," Amaya said. "What kind of burglar breaks

into an apartment and then ignores a giant stack of cash?"

Simon frowned. The more they learned about the case, the more confused he was. Something about the situation was not adding up.

in the garden

When Simon woke up the next morning, there was one thing on his mind. Their investigation had led to one dead end after another. He was tired of feeling like he was beating his head against a wall. He needed to talk to Mrs. Kobayashi.

The morning was sunny and bright, so he figured she might be in the garden. When he stepped outside, he almost bumped into a ladder.

"Watch it!" At the top was Oscar, holding a light bulb. He glowered at Simon.

"Sorry," Simon said, stepping to the side.

Oscar muttered under his breath, shaking his head. Simon scooted away as fast as he could. Just as he had hoped, Mrs. Kobayashi was working in a garden row.

"Good morning," she called. "How's your investigation going?"

"Not so great," he answered.

A lot of adults would start asking questions right away about what was wrong, but not Mrs. Kobayashi. She patted the gardening stool next to her, nodding at the raised containers. "These beds have weeds. Take care of them while we talk."

Simon arranged himself on the seat and began hunting for the tiny sprouts that didn't belong. Mrs. Kobayashi hummed quietly while she worked—a gentle, pleasant tune that made Simon feel relaxed. It was peaceful out in the courtyard. Oscar was far enough away that he wasn't there.

He pulled a few stubborn weeds, checking to make sure their roots stayed attached. Then he sighed deeply. "The case isn't working out. I think maybe we should just give up."

Mrs. Kobayashi glanced at him. "Why do you want to give up?"

Simon sighed. He would have to think of a way to explain without sharing specific details—otherwise Amaya would be mad.

"We keep trying to find out new information," he said. "But every time we do, it seems like we just have more questions."

157

"Sometimes pushing isn't the answer. Sometimes it's best to wait and watch," Mrs. Kobayashi said. "That's part of why I love gardening so much. All you can do is set up the right conditions. Make sure there's water and sunlight; make sure there's enough room to grow. And then you sit back and let it happen."

He dug at a particularly stubborn weed. "That might work on another kind of case. But we don't have time. If we don't solve it, my parents are going to make us move away."

Mrs. Kobayashi looked at him with kind eyes. "You want to solve the crime so you can stay here. Is this place that important to you?"

Simon brushed his hands on his shorts, thinking. "It's not perfect here or anything like that. But we're here, and I like it. It has stuff that Mom and Dad would like, too, if they'd give it a chance. But they're so worried after the burglary, it's like they're already planning the next place instead of making this one work."

She tilted her head. "Have you tried talking to them?"

Simon thought back to the conversation with Dad the night they'd met Calvin. He'd tried to explain how he was tired of moving, but Dad hadn't seemed to understand.

"Your parents care about you. Make sure your feelings aren't a mystery to them," Mrs. Kobayashi said.

He sighed deeply. "If I can just figure out this case, then everything will make sense."

Mrs. Kobayashi laughed. "Once a case gets its hooks in you, it's very hard to disengage. Be patient and allow yourself to observe. You may be surprised about the answers that appear when you aren't looking quite so hard."

Simon was turning over her words in his mind when a voice on the other side of the courtyard interrupted his thoughts.

"I need to know what kind of operation you're running here. It's abundantly clear that someone was in my apartment while I was out yesterday. When I saw footprints on the floor, I assumed you were there to fix the leaky faucet that I've been asking you about for weeks. But today, it's still leaking."

The man in the lavender suit—Amaya had said his name was Lorenzo—was face-to-face with Oscar. Lorenzo was so angry, even his face looked slightly purple.

Oscar scowled. "I told you I would let you know when I could schedule your repair. *I* wasn't in your apartment. Besides, I always wear shoe covers whenever I do service calls."

Lorenzo sniffed. "Perhaps it was one of the handymen. I know for certain someone was rummaging through my personal effects, because several items were out of place."

Simon took in a sharp breath. If someone had been in Lorenzo's apartment, maybe that meant that Lois and Roger weren't imagining things.

Oscar climbed down from the ladder. He crossed his arms stubbornly. "It's on the list. We're extremely short-handed at the moment."

Lorenzo sputtered angrily and let loose with a tirade. It was hard to understand where one word ended and the next began.

Mrs. Kobayashi frowned. "Some people are very difficult."

Simon nodded. "Oscar is pretty mean."

Her eyebrows shot up. "Oscar? Under that gruff exterior, the man is a giant teddy bear. I meant the other one—Lorenzo."

The door to the building opened, and Leah and Fin came out with Dolores. Fin's orange shirt had a stain down the front like he'd already found some mud to splash around in. Leah's babies rode in a stroller, and she happily pushed them in wide circles around the garden. Veronica came through the door holding a yoga mat. When Lorenzo saw her, he stopped mid-word and turned to her with a smile. His voice suddenly sounded smooth and buttery with no trace of the rage that had been there a moment before.

Mrs. Kobayashi's eyebrows drew together. "I'm wary of people who turn their charm on and off, like there's a switch."

When Veronica finished talking with Lorenzo, she headed toward Simon and Mrs. Kobayashi. Her gold bracelet glittered as she raised her hand in greeting. "Good morning!"

"Hi," Simon said.

Mrs. Kobayashi pointed at the big tree. "Is that your water bottle? I thought it looked familiar."

Veronica smacked her forehead lightly. "Thank you—I didn't even realize it was missing! Sometimes I think I'd lose my head if it wasn't attached."

Leah pulled at Veronica's leg until she obliged, leaning over the baby stroller and cooing at the dolls. When Leah was satisfied that Veronica had admired them sufficiently, she continued walking around the garden.

Simon returned to the weeding, thinking about Mrs. Kobayashi's words. He was willing to be patient, if that's what it took. He would wait and watch. But it would help a whole lot if he had the slightest clue what he should be watching *for*.

CHAPTER 22

not as easy as it looks

The next day, the doorbell rang.

When Simon answered it, Calvin was leaning on the wall, spinning a Frisbee. "Want to throw?"

They took the elevator downstairs. As they stepped out, Chef Jordan hurried on, holding a giant bag in her arms. She turned sideways so Simon couldn't read the label, but there seemed to be a ferret on the package.

Simon tilted his head for a better look, but Jordan jabbed at the button to close the doors.

Ferrets were allowed in the Tangerine, so there was no reason for Jordan to be so secretive. Simon wanted to discuss it with Calvin, but Amaya would never allow it. Besides, Calvin was already explaining the finer points of ultimate. It sounded much more complicated than

Simon had thought it would be. His palms began to sweat as he pictured the way it might go.

Swipe. Simon missing every single catch.

Swipe. Simon throwing the Frisbee in Mrs. Kobayashi's garden or on the roof of the shed—anywhere but in Calvin's direction.

Swipe. Calvin not wanting to be Simon's friend anymore.

By the time they got down to the courtyard, Simon's stomach was tense, and his heart was beating fast. He wondered what Amaya would do in the same situation. Probably, she would offer Calvin some shriveled grapes. She'd be talking so fast that Calvin couldn't get a word in edgewise. She never seemed to worry about what other people thought.

Simon wanted to be like that, too.

Calvin balanced the disc on its edge in the palm of his hand. "Most people start with a backhand, but it could be awkward on crutches." He demonstrated by throwing a perfect arc across the courtyard. He put his whole body into it, pivoting gracefully.

Calvin jogged to where the disc had landed, then returned to Simon's side. "See how I twisted my body when I was throwing?"

Simon nodded. "I might fall over if I tried that."

"Here's another throw that might work better before your cast comes off." Calvin held the disc with two fingers on the bottom and his thumb on top; then he snapped his wrist forward. The Frisbee landed a foot or two away from where it had been before.

"This throw takes a long time to get right," Calvin said. "But it's a good one to learn."

Simon nodded. "Sort of like skipping a rock."

Calvin handed the disc to Simon. "Exactly—now you try."

Simon held the disc and tried to copy Calvin's movement. It landed a few feet from them.

Simon's cheeks flushed. "That was a lot harder than it looked."

"You're doing great," Calvin said. "Let me show you how to straighten it out."

He moved Simon's fingers to adjust his grip.

Calvin held his hands, ready to catch.

Simon bent his arm at the elbow and snapped his wrist. The disc went farther, but it didn't go to Calvin. It landed in Mrs. Kobayashi's cucumbers.

Calvin sprinted to get it and came back in a flash. "Okay, try again."

The summer heat was rising. Simon wiped his sweaty palms on his shorts. His eyes narrowed in concentration.

He threw the disc at a bad angle—it almost hit Calvin in the knee, but he caught it at the last second.

Calvin smiled. "That's better."

Simon groaned. "I'm so bad at this. Probably anyone else would do better than I am."

Calvin held his hand up to block the sun. "Not me—I needed about two hundred times to get it right."

Simon's eyebrows popped up. "Two *hundred* times? Didn't you want to quit?"

Calvin shrugged. "I wanted to get better more than I wanted to give up."

He held out the disc, and Simon took it.

"You've done three throws so far. One hundred and ninety-seven to go," Calvin said.

Simon paused. "One hundred and ninety-seven to go until what?"

Calvin's eyes twinkled. "Until you can complain!" He held up his hands like a target.

Simon aimed and threw. It bounced off the garden shed. He winced, but Calvin retrieved it patiently.

"Four down," he said, giving the disc back.

Simon took a deep breath. He threw it again and again—sometimes hitting the ground, sometimes hitting the tree or a shed, and once, somehow, hitting himself in the chin. But he kept going.

It finally clicked around throw number 182. A perfect flick, right into Calvin's waiting hands.

"Yes!" Calvin shouted, looking so happy that he almost dropped the disc.

They began to do trick shots, making a game of trying to hit the tree trunk, the base of the fountain, and the side of the garden shed. Then they improvised a game where Simon stood in front of the fountain, swinging a crutch to block Calvin's shots. Then Simon sat on the garden stool and threw the disc while Calvin blocked Simon's shots. They easily got to three hundred throws apiece. Simon's hair was soaked through with sweat, and his arm ached. But he was happy.

He threw the Frisbee again—it soared perfectly above Calvin's head and landed in the fountain.

"Augh!" Calvin yelled, and both boys started to laugh.

If his parents had been there, they would have made a big deal of things. They would have snapped a photo, beautifully silhouetted against the sunlight. But that picture wouldn't have shown the two hundred attempts that Simon made before that one perfect throw.

His phone buzzed.

"Hang on," he called to Calvin. "Let me check my phone."

Calvin shook the Frisbee, drops of water flying every-where. "Take your time. Really."

Simon laughed, pulling the phone from his pocket.

> Where are you
> I found out something new.

> Busy right now will text later

Simon's smile disappeared. If Amaya found him with Calvin, she would be furious. He didn't plan to lie to her, but he also didn't want to tell her over text. He shoved the phone back in his pocket and neatly caught Calvin's forehand.

They played for another hour. By the time they were finished, the sun was high in the sky, and they were both sweaty. Except for the time he'd checked his phone, Simon hadn't thought once about Amaya or the necklace. It was nice to have a break from being serious.

When they stepped inside the lobby, Calvin was jok-ingly debating over the point that Simon had made to tie the score. The front door opened, and Ginger and Bianca came inside. They both seemed happy to see the boys.

Simon and Calvin leaned down to pet the dog.

"Good girl," Simon said. Her belly was bulging.

Ginger smiled. "I thought she would enjoy sitting out in the shade for a bit, but it's really too hot for her to move around much, sweet doggie."

Calvin asked about the puppies and said that he would ask his dads if they could have one. Simon tried to push down a pang of jealousy. He wanted to be happy for his friends. But before he could say anything, there was a scream from above.

"Help, help! There's been another robbery!"

Simon and Calvin stared at each other in confusion. Ginger looked shocked, too, but had the sense to spring into action. She scooped up Bianca and hurried for the stairs.

"How could this happen? It's not possible!" she cried.

Simon felt frozen. He looked at Calvin, who didn't seem to know what to do, either. But a few moments later, they heard Ginger shout.

"Get Oscar—it's Veronica's apartment on the second floor. Her gold bracelet is missing!"

CHAPTER 23

another break-in

Simon hustled to keep up with Calvin, who was nice enough to take the elevator with Simon instead of rushing ahead.

As the elevator went up, he could feel his stomach sinking down to basement level. *Another break-in.* Mom and Dad were going to be really worried when they found out.

When he exited the elevator, they followed the voices to Veronica's apartment. The front door was wide open. Oscar was on the phone.

"My bracelet!" Veronica sobbed.

"I'd like to report a theft," Oscar said into the phone, his voice a deep rumble.

Ginger poured her a glass of water, and Veronica took it gratefully.

"I can't believe it's gone. It's so precious to me," she wailed.

Ginger's eyes narrowed. "Was it insured? Prepare yourself to wait awhile for the money from the insurance company. They're *incredibly* stubborn. I should know—I've been through it all with my necklace, the Magnificent."

Veronica waved her hand. "I don't care about the monetary value. I just wish I could have it back. It belonged to my grandmother."

She took a long sip of water and then seemed to settle a bit. Ginger handed her a tissue, and she wiped her eyes.

Simon thought about what Amaya would do if she were here. She would ask questions. Simon would have to do that, too.

He turned toward Veronica. "Can you tell us exactly what happened? When did you notice it was missing?"

She pointed at a ceramic bowl on a table near the front door. "After yoga, I always come upstairs to get cleaned up and I put my bracelet here. I did that today, like normal. Then I went out for some errands, but when I got back to my apartment, the bracelet was missing."

"Was your front door unlocked?" Calvin asked.

Veronica shook her head. "I lock it every time and always check before I leave."

"You should look around to see if anything else is

missing," Ginger said. "And I'm going to tell my insurance company that there's been a rash of break-ins here at the Tangerine Pines. It seems like something very strange is happening here."

If Simon wasn't mistaken, Ginger was looking straight at Oscar when she said that.

He wandered back to the front door, not exactly sure what he was looking for. There were no scratches on the lock like there had been at Roger and Lois's. The door and frame were both in perfect shape, without even a speck of dust or a smudge anywhere Simon could see.

Calvin sidled over to him. "What are you doing?"

"I'll explain later," Simon whispered back—but it was too late. Oscar had noticed them, and he was frowning deeply.

"Better not touch that," he barked, holding his hand over the phone's speaker. "You're going to mess up the fingerprints."

Simon stepped back. "We aren't touching anything. We're just *looking*."

"Go on," he said. "You shouldn't be loitering here."

Ginger clicked her tongue. "Oh, Oscar. Don't scold them—they've done nothing wrong."

Oscar made a *hmph*ing sound and returned to his call.

Ginger picked up her purse. "I'm leaving, too—Bianca needs rest. I'll check on you later, Veronica."

Simon, Calvin, and Ginger headed down the hall, pausing in front of the elevators.

"Sorry that Oscar was so hard on you," she said. "I know you were just trying to help."

Simon's shoulders slumped. "I take back everything I said about him being nicer. He's just exactly as mean as he was the day I first met him."

Ginger tilted her head to the side. "You mentioned that before . . . what exactly happened the day you met Oscar?"

It felt like so long ago. He scrunched his forehead, thinking back. "It was the day we moved in. It was the same day your necklace got stolen, actually. Oscar was mad about the mail room."

Calvin nodded. "Oh, he's really picky about that. We had a book subscription service that mailed us boxes each month. He tried to say the packages were too heavy, so he was going to send them back. My dads filed a complaint."

"I just wish he wouldn't yell all the time," Simon said. "It's unnecessary."

Ginger's eyes widened. "Wait—why would he yell at you? You'd barely even moved in."

Simon shrugged. "It didn't make a lot of sense, but he blamed my family for the junk mail bin. He said it was because we forwarded our mail too early."

Ginger took a deep breath. "Where's that stack of mail now?"

Simon tilted his head, thinking. That day felt like ages ago. He hadn't thrown it away—he'd placed it all in his backpack so he could carry it upstairs. But he hadn't seen it since.

His backpack. Amaya had dumped it in his closet so they could carry the recording equipment. Because he stored his clothes in his dresser, he never used the closet, which was why he hadn't remembered.

"It's in my room," he said finally. "It was just a bunch of junk, though. Dry cleaning coupons and things like that."

Ginger looked like she wanted to say something, but she stopped herself. She shook her head. "Just between us, I've never trusted him. He's notoriously unpleasant. There's no reason to be so upset about mail, of all things."

She said goodbye to the boys and continued down the hall with Bianca, who waddled along happily.

Simon's wheels were spinning. People were complicated. But sometimes the truth was right there in front of your eyes. Mrs. Kobayashi had said it was better when people didn't turn their charming personality on and off. Oscar didn't have that problem—he was grumpy *all* the time.

And Simon didn't trust him one bit.

CHAPTER 24

a difference of opinion

> Veronica's bracelet was stolen!!

> WHAT. I will be right over.

Within moments, there was a tap at Simon's window. He pushed back the curtains and saw Amaya's grinning face.

"You could make it a lot easier on yourself if you left this thing open," Amaya said. "Although, now that I think about it, maybe that isn't the smartest idea with a thief on the loose."

Simon smirked. "I have a feeling that it doesn't matter one bit—he could get in if he wanted to. Because the thief has a key to every lock in the entire building. "

Amaya's eyes rounded. "What do you mean?"

Simon explained everything that had happened that day with Veronica's missing bracelet. Amaya nodded and said "mm-hmm" in all the right places, but it seemed like her enthusiasm lowered with every word Simon said.

"I don't know," she said finally. "It sounds like Oscar was being grumpy, sure. But why do you think he was involved?"

"Don't you see? There weren't any scratch marks on the lock. He didn't have to pick the lock because he already has the key. It happened in the short time she was gone doing that errand—and who knows the comings and goings in the building better than anyone?"

"Oscar does," she admitted. "I'm just not sure about the scratch marks, though. It doesn't sound like a real thing to me."

Simon spun slowly in his chair. He had thought Amaya would have been just as excited as he was.

He cleared his throat. "What was the thing you wanted to tell me?"

Amaya's eyes lit up. "Remember how I said that Three Pines sounded familiar? I looked them up. It's a company that buys real estate all over Rigsby, including the Tangerine Pines. They used to own the buildings on either side, too, but sold the properties a while back."

Simon scrunched up his face, thinking of the fancy house on one side and the tall apartment building on the other. "Is Ginger somehow a part of that company? No, that wouldn't make sense. She said that apartment building was an eyesore."

Amaya shrugged. "Maybe there's another explanation. It's interesting, though, don't you think?"

He frowned. "I think Oscar is involved somehow. There's something off about him—I don't know why you won't admit it. Even Ginger noticed the way Oscar was yelling at Calvin and me."

Amaya sat up straight. "*Calvin?* Calvin was there with you?"

Simon inwardly winced. It wasn't that he was keeping his friendship with Calvin a secret. It was that the timing wasn't the best to let Amaya know.

"We were throwing a Frisbee in the courtyard before it happened," Simon said.

She put her hands on her hips. "Are you two becoming friends or something?"

Simon frowned. "What is your problem with him, anyhow? He seems really nice."

Amaya's eyes flashed. "I already told you! He's a friend stealer. I used to be really good friends with the kid who used to live in this apartment, Riley. But as soon as Calvin moved in, they started leaving me out all the time."

"That stinks," Simon said. "But . . ."

Amaya raised an eyebrow. "But what?"

Simon cleared his throat. "Well—I wasn't here then, so I don't really know. But if Riley picked Calvin over you, isn't that more of a Riley issue? Maybe Calvin didn't know that you and Riley were friends. It sounds like Riley was the one leaving you out."

Amaya crossed her arms. "You're right."

"I am?" The words sounded friendly, but her voice sounded tight and angry.

"Just about the first part—when you said you weren't here, so you don't know. You don't know a single thing about it, Simon. But you started to investigate the new theft with Calvin. That was supposed to be our project!"

Simon held his head in his hands. This whole conversation felt like it was spiraling off in a direction that was way out of his control. "Amaya, I'm sorry. Our project is super important to me—I didn't plan for Calvin to be there. He ran for Oscar when Veronica screamed. What was I supposed to say?"

Amaya was quiet for a while. Then she nodded grudgingly. "All right. I can see how that might have happened."

Simon sighed in relief. "Okay, good. And maybe you

could give him a chance? We should try to get along—we all live in the same building."

Amaya bit her lip. "About that . . . I actually don't."

Simon was confused. "Don't what?"

She twisted a lock of her hair. "I don't . . . live in the building," she said in a small voice.

Simon squinted. "What do you mean?"

"I live next door," she said in a small voice.

He turned his head to look at the high-rise. "There? The place with the loft apartments?"

She shook her head. "The other side. The house."

Simon's eyes goggled. "You live in the *mansion*?"

"Sometimes people are weird about it," she said. "The money thing. So when you assumed I lived in the building, I—"

He folded his arms. "You lied."

Amaya paused. "Is it *really* a lie? I don't think so; I just let you think something else."

Simon's cheeks felt hot. "That's *lying*, Amaya. What about your big speech about how we are supposed to be a team? Are you even a pet sitter, or was that a lie, too?"

Amaya leaned forward. "I *am* a pet sitter. You know, I'm here so much, it's almost like I live here. This shouldn't be a big deal."

"I don't think you get to choose what's a big deal for me," he said. "I'm the only one who can decide that."

She took a deep breath. "Fine—but you lied, too."

Simon sighed. "Right. You already told me how you felt about Calvin."

Amaya shook her head. "Not that. You told me that you had lots of friends in the last place you lived, and I know that's not true."

Simon bit his lip. He had forgotten about his fib. It had been so long ago. He hadn't wanted her to feel sorry for him with having to move. And it hadn't hurt anyone. But it seemed like she'd never believed it for a second.

She nodded knowingly. "I can see by your face that I'm right. Do you want to know how I knew? You said you broke your leg. Then you said your friends had a big going-away party for you."

Simon scowled. He was in too deep to back down. "Okay, and?"

Amaya's eyes were bright. "And you don't have a single signature on your cast."

Simon looked down at his leg. Except for some dirt around the edges, the cast was a solid expanse of bright green.

"I want you to go," he said without looking up.

"Don't do that," Amaya said. "You lied and I lied. It's even."

He spun in his chair so he wouldn't have to see her. "Just go, Amaya, please."

Amaya was quiet for a long time. Simon watched her out of the corner of his eye. She picked up one of the rocks from his collection—an agate—and turned it slowly in her hand.

"You always talk about these rocks," she said. "You said they connect you to all the places you've ever been. But the place isn't what matters, Simon. It's the people. But I guess you don't care as much about that."

Amaya returned the rock to the bookshelf and went out the window. She pulled it shut with a rattle. Her steps trudged upstairs on the metal ladder. Eventually, it was quiet again.

Simon couldn't believe that so much could go wrong in a single day. He pulled out his collection, running his fingers over the soft, smooth, bumpy, and rough textures. He held them up to glint in the light from his lamp. Amaya didn't understand. The rocks were important because they reminded him of how he'd changed every time he moved.

Maybe he should stop trying to find the thief. If he told his parents, they'd probably be more than willing to move again—they could start packing up boxes tomorrow.

But this case had grabbed hold of him, like Mrs. Kobayashi said. Not just the case—this *place*. His friendship with Calvin—and Amaya, too, if that could be patched up. Bianca with the soft ears who was about to have puppies. His room with the squeaky floorboards and all the different windows. The alphabet pancakes at the ABC Diner. He wanted to hold on to all of it.

Simon had made up his mind. If he couldn't fix things with Amaya, he would have to find the evidence himself.

CHAPTER 25

a phone call

At breakfast the next morning, the doorbell rang.

Simon was half-hopeful and half-afraid. Part of him wanted to see Amaya, but part of him was afraid. He slouched low in his seat. It would buy him more time if she couldn't spot him from the doorway.

"Good morning!" said a sweet voice. It wasn't Amaya after all—it was Ginger. "I just wanted to drop by with a little welcome basket for all of you."

"Oh, that's so kind," Mom said, taking the basket. "Won't you come in?"

Ginger followed Mom into the kitchen. "I meant to bring it by much earlier, but with the theft and everything that came after, I've been overwhelmed."

Simon waved at Ginger, who waved back. He couldn't help but notice that she seemed much more cheerful than she had over the past few weeks. She looked alert and refreshed, and every hair was perfectly in place. She seemed much more like the person he had met on the first day they'd moved in to the Tangerine Pines.

"We meet again," she said. Then, turning to Mom and Dad, she asked, "Did he already share about yesterday's excitement?"

Dad's eyebrows drew together. "What happened?"

Simon suddenly became very interested in the bottom of his cereal. He was not going to make eye contact with either of his parents.

"Veronica's bracelet was stolen," Ginger said breathlessly.

Mom gasped. "Another theft?"

"That's terrible news," Dad said.

She filled them in on everything that had happened while Simon continued to shovel cereal into his mouth.

"But please don't get a bad impression of our little city," Ginger said. "In fact, this basket will help you get to know it even better." She began to explain the different items in the basket, which contained an assortment of jellies, soaps, cookies, and nuts. Mom and Dad made appreciative noises.

Then Ginger pulled out an envelope. "This is a special gift certificate for the bistro around the corner. Now, this is completely my fault for getting you the basket so late, but unfortunately, it expires tonight. Do you think you'll be able to use it?"

Mom and Dad exchanged looks.

"We can definitely use it tonight," Mom said. "Thank you, Ginger, that's so generous of you."

Ginger clapped her hands together. "I'm so glad to hear it. They open at six PM, and I recommend that you get there on the dot, because they can get crowded later."

"We'll do it," Dad promised.

She said goodbye and waved to Simon again before heading out the front door.

"That was nice of her," Dad said. "We've met some great people here—I just wish they could solve whatever's been happening with the thefts."

Simon smiled to himself. He was hoping to do exactly that.

There was just one problem: without Amaya, Simon didn't know where to start.

He wished he could ask Calvin for ideas, but he and Malik had gone on a family trip and would be gone overnight.

Simon skulked around the courtyard, which was empty except for the little kids and their babysitter,

Dolores. He made a quick exit before Leah could ask him to play babies with her.

Then he went to the mail room to see if he could figure out where Lorenzo lived. It turned out that he lived in 4D, next to Calvin. Simon tried to get close enough to see if there were scratches on the lock, but as soon as he came near, Lorenzo poked his head out.

"Can I help you?" he asked.

Simon froze up. "Um."

Lorenzo waved his hand impatiently. "Out with it."

"Uh," Simon said.

"Are you looking for Calvin? He's next door."

Simon pasted on a smile. "Yes, that's it. Thank you!"

Lorenzo slammed the door. Simon stood in front of Calvin's apartment for a moment and then went down to the conservatory.

He stood in front of the painting of Tangerine Pines, the original owner of the building. She had a sly grin, almost like she was reminding him that he wasn't any closer to figuring out the thief. She was wearing an ornate necklace. It reminded him a little of the Magnificent, but it was made of orange stones. The reason he hadn't noticed it before was because their hue was similar to the shade of the woman's hair, and they had blended in. But up close, he could see the details.

Squeaky footsteps entered the lobby, accompanied by a rattling sound. Without thinking twice, Simon unlatched the panel and went inside the storage area. When he peeked through the screen, he saw Oscar pushing a wheeled bucket. He splatted a mop on the floor and began pushing it around.

Simon lowered himself onto a box. So he was spying on Oscar. His parents would be mad if they knew. Amaya would say he was being ridiculous. But Simon knew that there was something off with Oscar. He needed a way to listen undetected.

Oscar's cell phone rang, echoing through the lobby—it sounded like an old-fashioned telephone. He picked it up with a gruff "yeah?"

As he listened, his mopping slowed, then stopped. Simon held his breath. His hands were suddenly clammy.

"Oh," Oscar said. "Hi."

His voice was almost completely different—the sharp edges melted away. His tone was smooth and soft. It was the voice of someone who knew what he wanted.

"Mm-hmm. What about later today? I brought everything with me."

Oscar was quiet again, then said something in a low voice—one that Simon couldn't quite make out. He pressed his ear against the screen.

Bzzzzt! Bzzzzt!

Simon's phone vibrated against his leg. He fished it from his pocket, but his grasp faltered. The phone clattered to the ground. It continued to vibrate, but the sound was even louder against the solid floor.

BZZZZT! BZZZZT!

Simon froze, staring at the phone. It was just out of reach.

"Hang on a second," Oscar said. "I just heard something strange."

Squeak, squeak, squeak. Oscar was coming toward the conservatory.

Simon's brain started racing. If Oscar caught him, he would be in so much trouble. He had to get his phone back.

Learning over, he stretched his fingertips as far as he could. Seconds passed, and it felt like hours. But eventually, he had it! As soon as it was in his hand, the phone buzzed again. Simon cupped it in his hands to muffle the sound. He switched the ringer to off and shoved it deep in his pocket, hoping it would be enough.

Oscar glanced around the room, frowning. He put the phone back to his ear, picking at a few brown leaves on a potted ficus.

"Not sure what that was. Go ahead." He paused for a moment, then chuckled warmly.

Simon's brain felt like a computer having an error. There was no way this was the same grump Simon had known since the first day he moved in.

"Well—yes. I have the items, just as we discussed. I think you'll find them *very* interesting."

Simon's eyes widened. *The items?* He wouldn't be talking about Ginger's necklace and Veronica's bracelet right here in the lobby—would he?

Another pause.

"Perhaps this evening for the handoff? Today, six o'clock, in the courtyard?"

"Handoff" definitely sounded suspicious. Simon scooted closer. There was a long pause in which he strained to hear.

Oscar's voice dropped low. "Perfect. See you then."

He tapped the phone and shoved it back into his pocket. Then he began to whistle as he cleaned the floor.

Simon could barely breathe. When Oscar finished mopping, his squeaky footsteps retreated. Simon popped open the panel and entered the conservatory. He sank into one of the armchairs and looked at his phone. The earlier call had been a couple of texts from his parents asking what kind of ice cream he wanted from the store. It was a rookie mistake not to switch the phone off while he was hiding. Amaya would have never let that happen.

More than anything, he wanted to text her—but she

wouldn't understand. The phone call had been suspicious—he was sure of it. But he hesitated before texting her number. If they fought again, things between them would be even worse.

He could try Calvin. But he'd started this investigation with Amaya. She was the one he should finish it with.

> Amaya we need to talk

> Oscar was on a call he said he's meeting someone in the courtyard tonight at 6 meet me there if you can

> Please don't ignore me

Simon stared at his last text but couldn't bring himself to send it. He backspaced over it and shoved the phone back into his pocket. He would have to handle it himself.

Even if that meant being at the handoff tonight—alone.

CHAPTER 26

an act

"Oh no," Mom said. "I'm so sorry you aren't feeling well."

Later that afternoon, Simon lay on the couch with his hands over his eyes, groaning. He was feeling perfectly fine, but he needed an excuse to skip dinner if he wanted to catch Oscar.

He tried to make his voice sound weak. "It's my head. And my stomach. And a tickle in my throat. I'll stay here and rest. You should go to dinner without me."

Dad felt Simon's forehead. "Sounds like you're really sick. Maybe we should stay home."

Simon pulled himself to a sitting position. "No! You have to go!"

His parents exchanged looks.

He cleared his throat. "I mean, you *have to* because of

the coupon, remember? It expires tonight. And I can be by myself for a while. I'm eleven and a half years old."

"We would be just around the corner . . . ," Mom said, as if she were considering it.

"I'll be perfectly fine," Simon said. "I promise to call if anything happens."

Like, for example, catching a thief as he attempts to sell the stolen jewelry, he thought to himself.

Mom bit her lip. "Should I ask a neighbor to check on you? Maybe Mrs. Kobayashi or Ginger could drop by."

Simon grimaced.

Dad rubbed his chin thoughtfully. "Let's have Simon decide. He's getting older, and he's been pretty responsible."

This made Simon feel even more guilty about lying. But if he told them about what he'd overheard, there was no way they'd let him go investigate. This was the only way to catch the thief before the jewelry was handed off and lost forever. This was the only way to make sure they got to stay at the Tangerine.

The next few hours, Simon tried to keep up the act of being sick—but not so sick that his parents would be nervous and decide to cancel their plans. Watching the time tick by was agonizing. He kept replaying the phone call in his mind. *Who is Oscar planning to hand off the jewelry to, and what is he getting in return? Probably a big stack of money. Or maybe a briefcase of gold.*

Finally, his parents were ready for their dinner. Dad had changed into a button-down shirt and khakis, and Mom wore a dress with tiny flowers on it. But then he saw something that made him frown.

"Mom? You should wear the diamond earrings tonight," he said. "The ones Dad gave you."

Mom looked puzzled. Simon wouldn't normally make suggestions about what she wore. "You think so?" But she returned to the bedroom and put them on.

Simon breathed a sigh of relief. The earrings were important to Mom. Even if it was unlikely that Oscar would show up to steal them, it was better to make certain they were safe.

"You sure you'll be all right?" Dad asked quietly. "It's not too late to cancel."

"I'm good," Simon said. "You and Mom go have fun."

Dad rumpled Simon's hair. "Call us if you need us."

Finally, the door shut behind them with a click. Simon eyed the clock and waited for four entire minutes. Then he grabbed his crutches and jumped off the couch.

It was time to catch a thief.

a chance to hide (and seek)

Simon had to hurry. He wanted to get there before Oscar showed up so he could find a place to wait and watch.

His stomach twisted in knots the entire elevator ride. But once he got out to the courtyard, he breathed more steadily. No one else was there.

He looked from left to right. As he saw it, there were two choices for hiding places: behind the shed or on the far side of the tree. It was mostly a question of location. The shed was closer to the benches and the garden, but the tree was closer to the grassy area where kids liked to play.

Simon decided on the shed. Something felt right about picking the location closer to the benches. The shed was also closer to the stairs, so if he had to make a quick escape, he could do so. He patted the phone in his pocket once more and leaned against the shed to wait.

The evening was warm and pleasant, and cicadas buzzed nearby. The light from the lowering sun touched everything with its golden glow. It really was a different world back in the courtyard—away from the traffic noise on the other side of the building.

And then he heard it: *Squeak. Squeak. Squeak.* Oscar's footsteps came down the stairs and crossed into the garden.

Simon had chosen the right spot. He leaned forward, risking a peek.

Although Oscar still wore his squeaky shoes, he had changed out of his usual coverall and instead was wearing a blue shirt and a red-striped tie. He carried a leather satchel, which seemed to be the perfect size for hiding jewelry.

Slowly, Oscar lowered himself onto the bench. He sat there for a few moments and then jumped up, searching his pockets. He removed a bandanna to wipe his brow—but the sweat just seemed to pop up immediately. He mopped his forehead, then twisted the bandanna in his hands. Then he retrieved an old newspaper from his bag and used it to dust off the bench before sitting down again.

There was no way around it—that was a weird thing to do. He must be super nervous.

Oscar had jumped up again and was pacing in tight circles, squeaking with each step. Simon's heart pounded in his chest. If the man took just a few more steps, he would find Simon's hiding spot.

Then Oscar came to a sudden halt, looking at the steps to the building. He arranged his features into a smile.

Click. Click. Click.

The footsteps made their way closer, walking on the brick path.

Shsh, shsh.

Then the footsteps were cutting through the grass.

Simon couldn't risk a peek—not yet. There was a rolling sensation in his stomach like it was full of marbles.

Oscar stood straight.

"Hello," he called to the other person.

Simon tried to swallow, but his throat had gone dry.

"Good evening," said a familiar voice.

His stomach squeezed. *No. It can't be.*

He peered around the corner.

Standing next to Oscar was the one and only Mrs. Kobayashi.

a mysterious exchange

Simon retreated behind the shed, gasping for breath.

He concentrated on steadying his nerves. If he made a noise and gave away his location, he might never know the truth. Even worse, he might come to actual harm.

The murmurs of their voices reached him from where he stood.

"Such a lovely evening," Mrs. Kobayashi said. "Thank you for suggesting it."

"I wasn't sure what to think when you didn't come to the conservatory," Oscar said quietly.

She looked puzzled. "Did we have plans to meet there?"

Oscar scratched his head. "The note—didn't you leave it?"

She smiled. "It must have been one of your other admirers."

Oscar blushed. What in the world was going on?

Mrs. Kobayashi held a wicker basket and was unpacking items one by one. Simon squinted to see what they could be.

"This all looks delicious," Oscar said shyly. "I don't know where to start."

He picked up a sandwich and nibbled at it daintily. Mrs. Kobayashi poured two glasses of iced tea.

Their voices were on the quieter side, but Simon could hear every word. Oscar asked her how her garden was growing, and Mrs. Kobayashi gave him a long answer about the squirrels getting into the tomatoes. She asked him about his hobbies. They talked about the weather.

Oscar patted his mouth with a napkin. "I almost forgot!"

He rummaged in his leather bag. Simon inched closer, not knowing what to expect.

"Here we go," Oscar said. He handed something to Mrs. Kobayashi.

Her eyes lit up. "The gardening books—you remembered!"

Oscar blushed again, beaming back. "I hope you can use them."

Oh no. This wasn't a jewelry handoff at all. This was a *date*.

Simon's cheeks flamed red. He was spectacularly embarrassed. The one small good thing was Amaya hadn't shown up. She would have laughed her face off if she could see that his big, exciting moment had turned into two old people having a picnic.

He shuffled backward, making for the steps. He didn't care if they saw him. He just wanted to be back upstairs before his parents got home.

CHAPTER 29

an impossible tangle

Simon turned his key in the lock and pushed it open.

Perfect—the house was silent. Mom and Dad were still at their dinner. He latched the door behind him.

His brain felt like an impossible tangle of thoughts. Every time he tried to follow one thread, it looped back on itself, twisting and snarling with other bits of information. He had been so sure it was Oscar—so sure that he'd even felt suspicious of Mrs. Kobayashi when he saw her. But he'd been wrong. Everything was all messed up with Amaya. He'd thought he could trust her, but she'd lied. He didn't know what to think. He didn't know who to believe. At that moment, he felt even further from finding the thief than he had been the whole summer.

Simon leaned his crutches against the counter. Then

he opened the refrigerator door and hoisted the chocolate milk, hopping the few steps to the cabinet that held the glasses. He truly couldn't wait to get his cast off. He was tired of being stuck in the building. He was tired of it taking so long to do simple things, like pouring himself something to drink.

Krr-squeak.

Simon froze. He would have known that sound anywhere. It was the creaky floorboard in front of his bedroom closet. Was someone in the apartment?

"Mom? Dad? . . . Amaya?"

There was no answer. He lowered the milk carton to the counter and grabbed his crutches.

His heart thumped as he approached his bedroom door. It was cracked open—was that how he'd left it? He couldn't be sure. He swung it open and saw—

Nothing.

Nothing? He frowned, surveying the room. It all looked normal. The book he was currently reading was on the window-seat cushion. His swivel chair was next to the bed, which had been made somewhat sloppily—typical for Simon, especially when he was doing it with one good leg.

A pizza coupon was on the floor in front of Simon's closet.

He looked at it, puzzled. That was odd. He *never* used that closet. It was much easier to keep his clothes in the dresser, because he could sit on the swivel chair and still reach everything.

Simon felt a chill. At first, he thought it was because he was nervous. But when he spun around, he saw the gentle swaying of the curtains on the window to the fire escape.

A breeze was coming through the open window.

Simon knew it was closed after his argument with Amaya the night before.

His stomach did a triple flip. Simon hated heights. But he had to know what was going on.

Before his brain had the chance to stop him, Simon crossed to the window and crawled onto the fire escape. He couldn't believe what he saw next.

CHAPTER 30

a (fire) escape

Halfway down the fire-escape stairs was a woman with red hair wearing a polka-dotted dress.

The stairs were steep enough that he was looking at the top of her head. But he didn't need to see her face to know who it was.

Still, Simon was confused. "Ginger?"

She froze for a moment. But by the time she looked up at him, she was grinning cheerfully. "Hello, there!"

In one hand she carried a manila envelope. When she saw Simon looking at it, she moved it behind her.

Simon tilted his head to the side. "What are you doing?"

Ginger tucked a curl behind her ear. "Oh, I was just having a little look at the view. It's so pretty out here.

Now, if you'll excuse me, I'll be heading back to my apartment."

Simon scooted to the top of the steps. "What are you holding?"

She widened her eyes. "This? Just a little piece of junk mail—it's nothing really."

Junk mail. Like the pizza coupon on the floor.

"Did you . . ." Simon trailed off. No—it wasn't possible. Not Ginger. But he couldn't shake the feeling that something was very wrong. "Did you get that from my room?"

Ginger's smile faded. "I should be the one asking questions. Why would an envelope with *my* name be stashed away in *your* closet?"

Simon's stomach dropped. For some reason, Ginger suspected him of doing something wrong.

"I didn't know there was an envelope for you," Simon said. "That's the junk mail that made Oscar yell at me— the stuff I told you about before. It's been sitting in my closet for weeks."

Ginger scoffed. "Am I really supposed to believe that? You and your little friend Amaya have been snooping around this entire building, and you never once thought to look in your own closet? I thought you were smarter than that."

"Excuse me," said a voice from below. "We are exceptionally smart. The only mistake we made was trusting you."

Simon and Ginger looked down to see Amaya climbing the fire-escape stairs. She stopped at the second story and looked up at Ginger. With Simon at the top of the steps and Amaya at the bottom, Ginger was trapped in between.

He had never been happier to see his friend. "Amaya!"

"Greetings and salutations," Amaya said. She reached out a hand for the manila envelope. "I'll take that."

Ginger pulled it away from Amaya's reach. "It's personal—mail for me. It's illegal to tamper with official mail, you know."

Amaya rolled her eyes. "I can see from here there aren't even any stamps on it. Why don't you tell the truth for once in your life?"

Simon's mouth hung open. He couldn't believe Amaya would be so bold. But Ginger didn't seem shocked at all.

"Okay, okay," said Ginger. "You figured it out. Let's stay calm and talk this over—maybe we could all have some tea at my place?"

"The thing I can't figure out is why," Amaya said.

"Some things in life don't make sense," Ginger said sharply. "Some things in life are just plain unfair."

A thought clicked in Simon's brain. One, two, three girls in the painting. One, two, three buildings in a row. The name on the records for Ginger's apartment: Three Pines.

"You said the youngest kid always gets left out," Simon said, remembering Ginger's comment from the day they interviewed her. "This building belongs to your family, doesn't it?"

By the way Ginger breathed in sharply, he knew he was right.

"It's supposed to be *mine*," she hissed. "My great-aunt promised to leave it to me—along with the Magnificent. Clementine and Olive got their necklaces *and* their buildings—they couldn't wait to sell them off immediately. But mine was declared *historically significant.*"

As she spoke, Ginger's face reddened until it almost matched her hair. She stomped her foot on the metal stairs and made a clanging sound. "They were never going to let me sell it. 'Think of the family memories, dear Ginger. Think of the painting of Auntie Tangerine in the lobby.' Easy for them to say—I didn't want to collect rent for the rest of my life—I needed a big chunk of money, just like Clementine and Olive got."

Simon was shocked, but Amaya simply shrugged.

"I couldn't stop thinking about the black-and-white

photo in her apartment—the one that showed all three buildings in a row," Amaya explained. "It's hard to tell now, of course, but back then they were very similar. I looked up the records on the sale of my parents' house and saw that the previous owner was named Olive Pines. I guessed that Clementine's building got sold to developers. But I couldn't understand why this one was still around. I figured somebody cared about it—had a special attachment and wouldn't want to sell it to just anyone."

Ginger sneered. "That's where you're wrong. If it hadn't been for my sisters, I would have sold it immediately after Auntie Tangerine died. Instead, I had to get creative. The insurance money on the Magnificent would give me what I needed, until the day I could sell this place."

"You faked the theft," Simon said. "But how did it get in my closet?"

A smile curled across Ginger's face. "Before I pulled the fire alarm, I hid the envelope with the necklace in the junk-mail bin. I knew that my apartment would be searched and it wasn't safe to leave it there. It was a huge stack of envelopes and flyers—no one ever looked through it."

"Except the next morning, I cleaned it out," Simon said. "I didn't even realize the envelope was there."

Ginger nodded. "When I checked the bin the next morning, it was empty. I figured it had to be someone in the building who had it."

"That's why you had so many questions about what other people were doing," Amaya added. "And that's why there were so many break-ins. You were trying to find the necklace."

"You're right," Ginger admitted. "I knew from the list that no one had gone in or out. I knew it had to be here somewhere! It wasn't until you mentioned Oscar being 'mean' about the junk mail that I realized Simon might have it."

Simon's brain spun. "Oscar said Mrs. Kobayashi stood him up. But you were the one who left the note to meet in the conservatory—not her."

Amaya clapped her hand to her forehead. "That day I dumped out your backpack, Simon—to make room for the recording equipment. I never thought to look to see what was in there."

Ginger looked back and forth between Simon and Amaya. When she spoke, her voice sounded like sugar. "The three of us are pals, right? As long as we keep this secret, there's going to be a payout from the insurance company—a big one. I'd be happy to cut you both in for a share, as a way of saying thank you."

Simon looked at Ginger—the person he'd thought was his friend. His throat squeezed together.

"You had a home," he said.

Ginger looked puzzled. "What do you mean?"

His fists clenched. "You had a home. A real home. Here at the Tangerine. With people who liked you. And you have Bianca. And a whole apartment full of beautiful things. You could have even sold the necklace if you wanted the money—but you were greedy. You wanted it all."

Ginger rolled her eyes. "That's enough. I'm leaving."

"No way," said Simon.

"Not in a million years," Amaya agreed.

The sweetness in Ginger's face evaporated. "Do you really think the two of you could stop me?"

She turned to head down the stairs, and Simon saw his opportunity. He grabbed the envelope.

Ginger shrieked.

He crawled for his bedroom window, but Ginger seized his good foot and pulled him toward her.

"Give it back!" she shouted, but Simon held the envelope out of reach. He grasped the windowsill and held fast. His arms and hands were strong from the weeks of using crutches. He would not drop it, no matter what.

There were sounds of a scuffle below. Amaya was

trying to pull Ginger away. Ginger turned and kicked Amaya squarely in the stomach, and Amaya doubled over in pain.

"Don't let her get it," Amaya wheezed.

"I'm trying!" But it was almost impossible to manage. Ginger gripped his good foot and kept reaching for the necklace. Simon held it farther and farther away. She held him around his chest and pulled upward so he was almost standing. Simon pushed off with his good foot. He twisted his body, trying to keep the necklace away from her. He accidentally put his full weight on his broken leg, which shrieked with pain.

"Give . . . it . . . to . . . me," Ginger said, grunting with effort.

Footsteps sounded on the stairs below them.

"Hold it right there," said a familiar, authoritative voice.

"The police are on their way," said a second voice. "I advise you to release him immediately."

Ginger let go so fast that Simon couldn't catch his balance.

He fell down the stairs.

Everything went black.

a green room

The smell of air freshener and antiseptic made his throat tingle.

His head hurt. His legs hurt, too.

"Mom? Dad?"

The walls were pale green. A blur of lavender balloons floated near the bed.

"Simon." Mom's voice, soft and soothing.

"You're safe." Dad's voice, warm and steady.

A glass vase bursting with purple blossoms was next to the bed.

His eyelids were *very* heavy.

Mom squeezed his hand. "It was a bad fall, but the nurses and doctors are taking care of you. You'll be okay."

Thoughts bubbled in his brain, but he couldn't match them with the correct words.

Amaya. Ginger. The necklace!

He tried to keep his eyes open. "We have to stop her."

In his mind, the words were sharp and crisp. But when he said them out loud, it was in a groggy murmur.

Dad arranged the pillow behind him. "Don't worry about that right now. You're safe."

Mom's cool fingers found his cheek. "You can go back to sleep."

Simon did.

CHAPTER 32

a pair of visitors

When Simon opened his eyes again, it felt like a thick fog had wrapped itself around his thoughts.

Earlier, his head had been screaming—but it had settled down to a dull roar.

Mom was right by the hospital bed. "How are you feeling?"

"Thirsty," Simon answered.

Mom helped Simon take a drink of juice. Dad came into the room carrying two coffees. When he saw Simon, he bounded over to the bed and pulled up a chair. "You're awake!"

Simon winced as pain sliced through his forehead. "What happened?"

Mom hesitated. "Do you remember?"

The memory of the day on the fire escape popped into Simon's head. "The necklace—Ginger took it! And I fell. Is Amaya okay?"

"She's perfectly fine," Dad said. "She's already visited several times. Calvin too. They'll be happy to hear you're awake."

"Who called the police?"

Mom smiled. "Mrs. Kobayashi and Oscar. Apparently, they heard the commotion from downstairs in the courtyard. They came to you right away—I don't know what would have happened if they hadn't."

"Ginger was arrested," Dad said carefully. "For insurance fraud, among other things. She won't be coming back to the Tangerine Pines."

"Her sisters called us," Mom said. "Olive and Clementine—they were very apologetic. Apparently, this isn't Ginger's first trouble with the law—which is why she didn't inherit the building in the first place. Now she never will."

Simon touched the bandage on his forehead.

"You got six stitches there," Mom explained. "And a concussion. And—"

Simon was already pushing back the bedsheet. Both his legs were in bright green casts. But this time, both were covered with signatures. Amaya and Calvin. Mrs. Kobayashi too. But also: Veronica, Lois and Roger, Hailey, Fin, Leah, and Rebecca, Lorenzo, Malik, and Jordan. Plus a bunch of names he didn't recognize.

"Some of the names are your doctors and nurses," Mom explained. "You'll meet them over the next few days."

Simon couldn't stop looking at the names. He couldn't help but stare when he noticed Oscar's signature in a thick, dark scrawl.

"Everyone from the building was worried," Dad said.

"Who are the balloons from?" Simon asked.

His parents exchanged glances.

"Lorenzo brought them—and the flowers," Mom said.

Simon's face scrunched. The man in purple? They'd barely spoken, and he had not been friendly. "But he doesn't like anyone."

Dad chuckled. "Not true. Apparently, Lorenzo is a big fan of The Hydes Go Seek. Since he made the connection, he's been very supportive."

"You've made a lot of friends in a short period of time," Mom said. "So many people care about you and want to be sure you're okay."

"What about Bianca and the puppies?" Simon asked.

"Mrs. Kobayashi is taking care of Bianca for now," Dad said. "The puppies will be born soon."

"Knock, knock," said a voice.

Amaya and Calvin burst into the room. He carried a

reusable bag patterned with goldfish, and she held a balloon in one hand and something purple in the other.

"Greetings and salutations," she said. "I brought you some amethyst because I know you like rocks and this balloon because that's what people in the hospital always get. Except it got dirty somehow on the way here. Probably because we had to take three different buses—we went north by northwest, then had to double back on the southbound express." She grabbed a tissue from the box on the counter and dabbed at the balloon, which drifted away each time she touched it.

Calvin handed the bag to Simon. "My pop said I should bring a plant, but I didn't think you'd want that. So I brought you candy instead."

Mom and Dad stood up.

"We'll let you have a little time with your friends," Mom said. "Does anyone want anything from the cafeteria?"

Amaya and Calvin shook their heads. After the door closed, they pulled their chairs closer. Simon opened the bag and spilled a brightly colored avalanche of candy onto the blanket.

"Nice," he said approvingly.

"Calvin got a decent selection," Amaya noted, grabbing some gummy worms. "Sour, fruit, chewy, chocolate."

Calvin unwrapped a peanut butter cup. "I'm a big believer in representing all the major food groups."

Amaya laughed, popping another gummy in her mouth. For a while, the room was quiet except for the sounds of chewing and crinkling candy wrappers.

Simon looked back and forth between them. "Are you two friends now?"

Calvin scrunched up his face. "Turns out it was more of a misunderstanding."

Amaya shifted in her seat. "I listened to what you said about the Riley thing. I maybe, *maybe* was a tiny bit jealous because so many people at school like Calvin."

Calvin shrugged. "People like you, too, Amaya."

Amaya's cheeks reddened. "Anyway. We started talking because we were so worried about you, Simon." She took a deep breath and scooted forward to the edge of her seat. "Are you okay? They said you would be fine, but are you *really?*"

Simon thought for a moment. His head still hurt. He had two broken legs. But he also had two friends who'd taken three buses to come visit him.

He grinned. "I'm really okay."

Amaya leaned back, relieved.

Calvin tapped on his own forehead in the same place where Simon's bandage was located. "Are you going to have a scar?"

Simon shrugged. "Probably not—they made really small stitches."

Calvin looked a little disappointed. "Well, it would be a good place for a scar if you end up having one."

Amaya bit her lip, smoothing a candy wrapper with her fingers. "It was scary after you fell. But Mrs. Kobayashi was amazing. She handcuffed Ginger until the police got there . . . with her own personal handcuffs!"

Simon's eyebrows popped up. "Do you ever get the feeling that Mrs. Kobayashi has had a lot more adventures than we imagined?"

Calvin nodded. "*Definitely*—she's really tough. I'm glad she's on our side."

At this, everyone cracked up. They filled in Simon about what had been going on at the Tangerine Pines the last few days. There had been a big meeting to talk about what Ginger had been up to. A lot of people were shocked. But there were a few people suggesting that the building do more so people could get to know one another. A book club had formed among the adults, and there was talk of a building-wide party to celebrate fall.

"Who were your other suspects?" Calvin asked.

Simon and Amaya exchanged glances.

"I thought it was Oscar," Simon admitted. "But I was wrong. He's grumpy, but he's not a thief." Simon explained about the way he'd hidden in the garden—how he'd been so confused when he saw Oscar with Mrs. Kobayashi.

Amaya jumped out of her chair. "I forgot to tell you—I found out something about Jordan. The building rules say you can only have two pets, but she has *four* ferrets. That's why she wouldn't help Mrs. Kobayashi during the fire alarm. She had to find a box that was big enough to hide all of them."

"Okay, that makes sense," Simon said.

"That's also the reason she never wanted me to pet sit," Amaya said. "I assume, anyway."

Calvin looked at her curiously. "Was she a suspect just because she didn't hire you to take care of her ferrets?"

Amaya shrugged. "You have to admit that it's highly suspicious. I'm an excellent pet sitter." She sighed deeply, tying her balloon to the side of his bed. "Did you ever think about who invented these? Aren't they weird? Is it something that happened before or after hot-air balloons? Who was the person who had an idea to make stretchy round things and put air inside them?"

"I think you mean *helium*," Calvin pointed out. "For that one, anyway."

Amaya nodded impatiently. "Okay, not really the point, but—okay. Helium. Regardless, people basically made bags and filled them with gas and put ribbons on them. Completely bizarre."

When Mom and Dad returned with their coffees,

Simon and his friends were in the middle of a game where they tried to launch the crinkly wrappers into the trash can in the corner of the room. The papers were lightweight and surprisingly difficult to throw, but that just made the competition more heated. And hilarious.

"Augh!" Amaya shouted. "That one was so close!"

"My turn!" Simon said. His throw somehow looped in the air and ended up *behind* him. They all started cracking up.

Mom and Dad entered the room. Simon didn't know if they were more surprised at the noise level or the layer of candy wrappers scattered across the floor.

"Okay, kids," Dad said. "Thanks so much for coming by. I think Simon's going to need some time to rest now."

Amaya and Calvin said goodbye and that they'd see him soon.

As good as it had been to see them, Simon had to admit that he was now exhausted. His eyelids felt incredibly heavy. He leaned back against his pillow.

Mom adjusted his blanket. "Those are some great friends. They really care about you."

"Simon always makes good friends." Dad reached over and ruffled his hair.

Simon frowned. He fought against the temptation to go along with what Dad had said.

"Not *always*," he said.

His parents glanced at each other.

"No one even signed my cast in the last place we lived," Simon said. "And no one's texted me this whole time."

"But it's summer," Dad protested. "Everyone's busy in the summer. It can be hard to find the time."

Simon shook his head—wincing, as he remembered too late that his head needed to heal before he could do that again. He cleared his throat. "Amaya and Calvin are busy, too. Amaya runs three businesses. Calvin plays all kinds of sports and helps coach a kindergarten basketball team. Some people wait to find the time, but a real friend will make time, no matter what."

He settled back in bed and rested his eyes, but he couldn't stop the thoughts from swirling in his head. "I want to live somewhere for a whole school year. Maybe two. I want to see Bianca and her puppies. I want to make it all the way through the menu at the ABC Pancake Diner. I'm only at G."

Mom adjusted his pillow. "Shh, Simon."

"I want to find more rocks," he muttered. "Lots of them. I want my collection box to be so heavy, we can't carry it."

"You need your rest," Dad said gently.

Simon's eyelids felt very heavy, but he had to make them understand. "I have a lot of stuff to tell you."

Mom brushed his hair back from his forehead. "Go ahead."

"The Hydes Go Seek," Simon said.

His parents exchanged looks. "You want us to stop?"

Simon shook his head, then winced. "You can keep doing it. But sometimes I want it to show the things that go wrong. The stuff that isn't always nice. I want it to look real, like we do normal things that aren't always on a top-five list."

"Got it," Dad said in an amused voice. "No top-five lists."

Simon forced his eyes open. "This is important."

"I know it is," he said. "We hear you—I promise."

Finally, Simon allowed his thoughts to drift, thinking about balloons and candy and garden picnics and heavy rocks and his very real friends at the Tangerine Pines. Then he fell asleep.

CHAPTER 33

a final mystery

"There's just one thing that's troubling me," Amaya said.

Weeks later, it was morning in the Tangerine Pines courtyard. Simon, Amaya, and Calvin sat under a tree—Simon in the wheelchair that he needed to use until he was done with his leg casts. Veronica did yoga. Fin balanced on a bench, Hailey dribbled a soccer ball, and Leah tucked her dolls into the baby stroller while their babysitter, Dolores, watched from underneath a nearby tree.

With a *skritch-skritch-skritch*, Simon scratched at the outside of his newer cast. It turned out that his left leg got just as itchy as his right leg had. He shifted in his chair to see if that might help. It didn't.

"What's bothering you?" Calvin asked.

Amaya twisted her hair into a bun. "We've solved almost every mystery. Obviously, the necklace was the biggest one—and Ginger confessed to all the break-ins except one," Amaya said.

"The one at Veronica's house," Simon said.

Calvin nodded. "There weren't any items stolen at the other break-ins—that's because Ginger was trying to find the Magnificent, which obviously was in your room the whole time. But who took Veronica's bracelet?"

A small hand pulled at Simon's arm.

"Play babies with me," Leah commanded.

Simon shook his head. "Sorry, Leah—"

"Princess Leah," she insisted.

Simon took a deep breath. "Princess Leah. Right now I'm busy, but maybe later—"

The little girl pushed a doll into Simon's arms. "*Now*. It is now time for the ball."

Amaya scooched backward, and Calvin suddenly pretended to be fascinated by something in the sky. They knew it was best to avoid eye contact or else be roped into an afternoon of playing dolls.

"Which one is she?" Simon knew better than to make assumptions.

"That's Baby Princess," Leah answered. She began to furiously brush at another doll's head. "Her fairy godmother made her a dress, and now she's at the ball. She likes to be fancy."

The doll's hair stuck out in many different directions. Her dress was shiny, with what Simon considered an excessive amount of ruffles. A slightly too-large crown was crammed onto her head, partially covering her eyes.

Something glinted around the doll's neck.

"Um," Simon said. "What's this?"

"That's her *jewelry*," Leah answered.

At this, Amaya raised her head. "Jewelry?"

Calvin leaned in for a closer look.

Wrapped tightly around the doll's neck was a chain made of gold links. Simon began to unwind it.

"No!" Leah howled. "No, that's her necklace because she's a princess! Her fairy godmother gave it to her!"

"I'm just going to look at it," Simon said.

Leah watched him, spellbound. Simon examined the clasp, which was broken.

"I think this is Veronica's bracelet," he said.

"That's what I said," Leah said. "Veronica is the fairy godmother."

"Tell us where you got it," Calvin said. "Did you find it on the ground?"

Leah shook her head. "Veronica said hi to this baby when she was in her stroller and when she was done I

found the jewelry which means she is going to the ball."
She seemed annoyed that the other kids were having
trouble grasping her logic.

Amaya pointed to one end of the bracelet. "The clasp
is broken. Maybe it fell off Veronica's wrist when Leah
was showing her the doll stroller."

Calvin scratched his head. "So it wasn't stolen this
whole time—it was *lost*."

Simon looked at Leah carefully. "We have to give this
back to Veronica. She thought it was lost, and she's very
sad."

Amaya waved Veronica over. When she saw what
Simon was holding, her eyes lit up.

"My bracelet! But where did you find it?" Veronica
asked.

Amaya explained that it had been Leah's doll's "jewelry." Simon showed Veronica the broken clasp before
handing it to her.

Veronica snapped her fingers. "I remember now! The
day it went missing, I had chatted with Leah about her
babies. I bet it fell off into the doll stroller. When I didn't
see it in its usual bowl, I assumed it was stolen like Ginger's
necklace. I guess no one broke into my apartment after all."

Leah's chin trembled, and a few tears rolled down
her cheeks. "But I *love* the fancy necklace."

Veronica hugged the little girl. "I'm so sorry, Princess Leah. I'll get you some new jewelry for your baby doll, okay?"

Leah wiped at her cheeks, suddenly clear-eyed. "A necklace *and* a bracelet?"

Veronica nodded. "I promise."

"And a purple pony?" Leah added. "And a baby fox?"

"Of course," Veronica answered before returning to her yoga mat.

Leah nodded firmly and ran off to play.

Amaya arched her eyebrows, impressed. "That is one smart and tough little kid."

Calvin tilted his head. "I guess it costs less than replacing jewelry. Veronica's just happy to have it back."

"You mean she's *lucky* to have it back," Amaya said. "If Leah hadn't wanted to return the bracelet, there was zero chance of it happening."

Simon shook his head. "Remind me never to bargain with a princess."

The three friends started laughing and couldn't stop.

CHAPTER 34

finding magnificent

It had always seemed to Simon that time sped up at the end of summer vacation, and that year was no exception. It may have seemed that way because of all the fun they were trying to squeeze in to the end of summer. Or it may have felt that way because there were so many big things that happened during that time.

Even though the mystery of the Magnificent was solved, Simon, Amaya, and Calvin still spent every day together. It turned out there was a lot to keep them busy. Simon was officially down to one cast, which made getting around a lot easier. Calvin had managed to teach him some more Frisbee throws, and there was a spot on the ultimate team waiting for Simon when he was out of the second leg cast.

Mom and Dad surprised him with a trip to a gem mine. They'd gotten a flat tire and, true to their promise, they actually posted about it. Not in a way where it was quirky and funny and cute, but in a way that went below the surface—one that was truthful about the fact that they'd all been annoyed, frustrated, and hot. But it had all ended well. They had a really good time and came home with a bucket of finds, plus some topaz earrings Mom bought from the gift shop. Simon had even found a tiny ruby of his own—just a chip, really. But it glowed in the sun, and he knew it would always remind him of the mystery that he'd solved with his friends.

The happiest news was that his parents had decided to give the idea of settling down in Rigsby a real chance.

"We've thought it over," Mom had said. "And we're going to give it a try."

Simon's eyes had widened as he looked back and forth between his parents. "Really? You mean it?"

Dad had nodded. "We want you to have some stability. Oscar offered us a two-year lease, and we took it. We'll find a way to have our adventures on school breaks, okay?"

"That's a deal." Simon's fingers were already itching to text Amaya and Calvin in their group chat. When he did, they were almost as excited as he was. Amaya was planning a new podcast they could work on, even though they'd never finished the first one. It was too soon to know if the Tangerine would really be a forever home, but it was already something extraordinary.

The most curious piece of news was that Ginger's apartment was about to be rented again. After she was arrested, her sisters, Clementine and Olive, came to visit with Simon, Calvin, and Amaya. First, they apologized for how Ginger had treated them and fussed over Simon's second broken leg. Even though Ginger had always felt like she'd gotten an unfair deal by being the youngest, it was obviously no excuse to act the way she did. Then they packed up Ginger's apartment and put all the contents in storage. They would be renting to a new tenant, but they assured Simon that no matter what, Ginger would not be coming back to the building.

The most *exciting* piece of news was that Bianca had finally had her puppies—three of them. Simon and his friends had wanted to visit right away, but the puppies were too small for a lot of excitement. Instead, Mrs. Kobayashi updated them with daily pictures. Their favorite picture was the one with Oscar holding all three of the puppies at the same time. He'd warmed up a whole lot over the past few weeks and had even given Simon a new rock for his collection—a cordierite, a mineral that changed color when viewed from different angles. In one direction, it was a yellowish-gray. But in the other, it was violet-blue. Simon thought that was a good fit for Oscar, who also seemed to be different when he was looked at in a new way. Sometimes a first impression was just that—a beginning. What really mattered was what happened in the rest of the story.

After what seemed like *forever*, the day had arrived when Simon, Amaya, and Calvin were going to meet the puppies in person.

As they stepped off the elevator, Amaya peppered Simon and Calvin with questions. The three of them had made cookies earlier that day, and she insisted on carrying them.

"Did you remember to wash your hands? Mrs. Kobayashi said that we couldn't bring in any germs or it could make the puppies sick. And remember, you'll have to take off your shoes and use quiet voices."

"We know," Simon said. "We read the same texts you did."

Amaya scrunched her forehead. "I'm sorry! I'm just really excited."

"Me too," said Calvin. "I can't wait to see them."

They knocked, and Mrs. Kobayashi opened the door.

"These are for you," Amaya said.

"We remembered the advice you gave," Simon said. "When in doubt . . . make cookies."

Mrs. Kobayashi beamed, peeling back a corner of the foil to have a look. "That's probably the best advice I've ever given. These look scrumptious."

"They're cherry double chip," Calvin added as they followed her inside.

"You three have perfect timing," she said. "The puppies just woke up from a nap. You can leave your shoes here in the hall and then come on in."

She had them all stop at the sink and use a special soap to rewash their hands and arms up past the elbow. Then they continued to the living room.

Mrs. Kobayashi moved a baby gate to the side so Simon and his friends could come through the gap.

"They like to explore and get into mischief," she explained. "If they stay in one area, it's easier to keep an eye on them."

Bianca was sprawled on the rug, and her puppies surrounded her. One was a silvery gray, with soft, rounded ears and a short coat. One was a deep honey color with pointy ears and a curly tail. And one was small and white, with a coat that was already beginning to look shaggy—just like Bianca.

"Hi there," Simon said softly.

Bianca thumped her fluffy tail as if to say, *See what I did? Aren't they wonderful?*

Amaya clasped her hands together. "They're so small."

"They're so *cute*," Calvin whispered.

"Go ahead and sit on the floor," Mrs. Kobayashi said. "Simon, I have a cushion that might make it a bit easier with your leg. Or you can sit on the sofa if you'd rather."

Simon wanted to be as close to the puppies as possible. With some help from Calvin and Amaya, he lowered himself onto a firm pillow.

At first, the puppies didn't pay them much attention. The silver one mouthed a knotted length of fleece material. The honey-colored one scampered over to him and grabbed the toy with his tiny teeth, trotting away as fast as his little legs could carry him. The silver one seemed confused for a moment but then followed—trying to get his toy back. Amaya and Calvin giggled, watching their antics.

Bianca approached Simon and put her head on his leg. He scratched behind her ears.

"You're a great mom," he whispered.

The white pup approached Simon, her tail wagging wildly.

Mrs. Kobayashi patted Simon's shoulder. "It's okay to hold her if you want to."

Simon didn't have to be told twice. He scooped her up in his arms and looked at her little face. Her eyes were warm and chocolatey, and her ears were silky. She cuddled up against his chest like they were old friends.

"She's perfect," he said, petting her softly.

"Do you want to hold one of the others? This one is very brave." Amaya nodded at the honey one, who was romping around a tiny squeak toy, occasionally biting it in the most adorable attack mode ever.

"This guy is really sweet, too," said Calvin, who was scratching the belly of the silver boy. The puppy's tiny tongue rolled out of his mouth, and he looked dazed with happiness.

Simon looked down at the white pup, who had fallen asleep in his arms. "I think this one is my favorite."

Amaya and Calvin exchanged looks.

Simon turned to Mrs. Kobayashi, who was folding a stack of towels. "Are you going to miss having the dogs when they go back to the rescue?"

Mrs. Kobayashi smiled, putting the laundry into the basket. "I've decided that Bianca is going to stay with me. I've grown attached to that sweet girl over the last few weeks. I will miss the puppies, but they won't be too far if I ever want to visit."

Simon's eyes widened. "That's great news—that

Bianca's going to be here still. Did you say . . . did you say you already have homes for the puppies?" He hoped his voice didn't sound too disappointed. He hoped they would stay at Mrs. Kobayashi's for at least a little while longer.

"*Well—*" started Amaya.

Calvin poked her arm. She clamped her hands over her mouth, as if she was trying to cram the word back down her throat.

"We aren't supposed to tell," Calvin said.

Simon looked back and forth between them. "What's going on?"

Mrs. Kobayashi's eyes sparkled. "I think it's okay to let him know."

Amaya sat up straight. "Long story short, you get to have one of the puppies, Simon. Any one you want."

Simon's jaw dropped open. "*What?*"

Calvin nodded. "After they were born, Amaya and I both asked our parents if we could have one. They said yes, but we didn't think it was fair to you if we got to have one and you didn't."

"We wrote a really long letter to your parents about it," Amaya said.

"And a PowerPoint," Calvin added. "Amaya also made a PowerPoint."

Amaya grinned. "Anyway, they ended up saying yes."

This must be a dream. Simon pinched his arm. Nothing happened. He was still holding a sweet, sleeping puppy. And his friends were looking at him expectantly.

"They wanted it to be a surprise," Mrs. Kobayashi said. "Your friends wanted you to have first pick, since you've been through so much this summer."

Amaya's eyes crinkled at the edges. "A second broken leg has to have *some* benefits—it's only fair."

Calvin tilted his head at the little white dog in Simon's arms. "She's your favorite, right? That's the one you'll keep?"

Simon could barely believe it. This little dog, so warm in his arms . . . was *his*?

Amaya rolled a tiny ball across the floor for the honey-colored pup, who chased after it in a frenzy. "What do you think you'll call her?"

Simon was quiet for a long time. He'd dreamed of having a pet for so many years, and of course he had some favorite names. Root Beer. Luna. Pearl. But none of them seemed quite right. He needed the perfect name. He needed a new name, one that would make sure he never forgot all the events of this summer.

Finally, he cleared his throat.

"I think I'll call her Magnificent," he said. "Maggie for short."

His friends grinned.

"Perfect," Calvin said.

"Aww, Maggie," Amaya cooed. "That's a good girl."

Simon could picture it.

Swipe. Amaya with the honey-colored pup and Calvin with the silver one.

Swipe. Simon, Amaya, and Calvin would learn to train the dogs and make sure they had good manners. They'd get the right food and collars and everything a dog could need.

Swipe. One day, after Simon's cast was off and the dogs had all their vaccinations, they'd be able to take them for a walk together—all six of them. Into the sunset. And they'd all be holding ice-cream cones. And the birds would be singing.

And . . . wait a minute.

His life wasn't a social media post. There were going to be messy parts, too. Like, for instance, teaching the puppies to pee and poop outside. That was practically the definition of messy.

And: sometimes friends argue.

And: sometimes you need two hundred tries before you get something right.

And: no place (or person, or friendship) is really *perfect*.

But still, it was time to leave Code Name Chameleon behind. Code Name Reality was a lot better.

His smile was so wide that his cheeks began to ache.

"Cookie?" Mrs. Kobayashi asked, passing him the plate.

Simon grinned, taking two. "Always."

Maggie stirred in her sleep. He patted her until she settled again.

As he chewed, he thought about the summer. The original goal had been to find out what happened to the missing ruby necklace. The investigation had led them in all directions, to all kinds of different people. They'd listened in on conversations and they'd put together clues. They'd made friends along the way. Even though he and Amaya had fought, she'd been there when it counted. They'd worked together to catch the thief—and it was because of them that she would stay in prison for a long, long time.

Simon looked around the room at his friends. His parents had surprised him. But Calvin and Amaya had surprised him, too—in the very best of ways.

His cast would be off soon. It was layered over again and again with signatures. At this point, everyone in the building had signed it at least once. Leah had added a few scribbles. (He had been informed it was a baby fox.) Amaya and Calvin had even played a few games of tic-tac-toe there. It was very, very different from the plain green cast he'd had at the beginning of the summer.

Life can be a mystery of its own. He and his family had traveled thousands of miles looking for something extraordinary. But Simon was learning that sometimes you had to stay close to home to find what was truly magnificent.

ACKNOWLEDGMENTS

Gauri Johnston, this one's for you. While I don't think you've ever climbed a fire escape to visit me, I know that you would have if I needed you to! My very first friend in St. Louis, you were there for me during one of the most difficult years of my life and you've been right there with me ever since—for all the highs and lows. I have no idea what I would do without our chats. I love you, my wonderful friend.

Marietta Zacker, thank you for the many conversations and emails and all the support. You are always the voice of reason and I am so lucky to have you in my corner.

Mary Kate Castellani, it was such a pleasure to work on this one together! I'm so happy that our shared love of mysteries could come together in a project. I'm thankful for the way you challenge me and help my books become the best that they can be.

Huge thanks to the teams at Bloomsbury and Gallt & Zacker Literary Agency. So many contributed to this book, especially Diane Aronson, Erica Barmash, Faye Bi, Erica Chan, Nicholas Church, Phoebe Dyer, Beth Eller, Alona

Fryman, Lex Higbee, Donna Mark, Kathleen Morandini, Kei Nakatsuka, Laura Phillips, and Lily Yengle. Special thanks to Kristin Sorra and Jeanette Levy for the wonderful cover, which fits the story perfectly, and to Ashlee Latimer at GZLA for the handholding and encouragement with my social media.

Camille Andros and Stephen Messer, you bring all the fun to my Tuesdays. Thank you so much for your feedback and support on this one.

Brigid Kemmerer, thank you for reading an early version of this. You are such a wonderful sounding board and I appreciate the way you encourage me to be brave and try new things.

Jackie and Dan Skahill, Anna Totten, Wendy Chen, Jen Shapiro, Julia Ellis, Andi Bradford, Kim Mullikin, Caroline Flory, Adrianna Cuevas, Chris Baron, Rajani LaRocca, Nicole Panteleakos, Naomi Milliner, Josh Levy, Cory Leonardo, Jessica Kramer, Jess Redman, Laurie Morrison, Jasmine Warga, Lisa Moore Ramée, Mariama Lockington, Jennifer Springer, Mandy Roylance, the Hemingway family, Ashley Bernier, and Sam Flynn . . . your friendship, encouragement, and support mean the world to me.

Teachers, librarians, booksellers, and reviewers—thank you for your work getting books into the hands of kids. I appreciate you!

Fin, Hailey, and Leah—three beautiful spirits that left us all too soon. Your families love you so much and continue to tell your stories. I am honored to have characters named after you.

Aislinn Estes, our time together this year meant the world to me. I'll always remember our amazing drive in the mountains—the scenery and the conversations. I love and appreciate you so much!

Nora, Leo, Olive—it is no mystery that you inspire me in everything I do. I couldn't be prouder of you or love you anymore. Thank you for our famchat, our travels, our movies and shows, the playlists, the recipes, our heated games of UNO Flip and Karma King, and for always being up for an adventure. I am so lucky to be your mom.

Friday, thanks for being the best dog, for being fairly quiet when I'm on video calls, and especially for curling up next to me when I'm feeling stuck.

Jon, you've been there for me through every twist and turn—in my books and in our lives together. Somehow you manage to make every day better. You're the kindest, strongest, and most generous person I know and I love you to pieces. I won the bingpot when I married you.